Twisted Ever After #1

A. Zavarelli

This book contains dark subject matter. Please read at your own discretion.

Copyright © 2017 by Ashleigh Zavarelli
Cover Design by Coverluv Design
Cover Photograph © 2016 Furious Fotog

All rights reserved.
No part of this book may be reproduced in any form or by any electronic or mechanical means, including information storage and retrieval systems, without written permission from the author, except for the use of brief quotations in a book review.

PLAYLIST

I Know You- Skylar Grey
Pretty When You Cry- Lana Del Ray
Lost Boy- Ruth B.
Bad Things- Jace Everett
I Put a Spell on You- Annie Lennox
Creep- Radiohead
Set Fire to the Rain- Adele
Run- Leona Lewis
Lift Me Up- Kate Voegele
Ultraviolence- Lana Del Ray
Roses- Carly Rae Jepson
Bird Set Free- Sia
How Long Will I Love You- Ellie Goulding
Hurts- Emeli Sande
Kingdom Fall- Claire Wyndham
Without You- Lana Del Ray
Gone Away- Noctura
All Around Me- Flyleaf
Dark Side- Kelly Clarkson
Lightning Crashes- Live
Something to Remind You- Staind
Over You- Miranda Lambert
See The Sun- Dido
Gods and Monsters- Lana Del Ray
A Sorta Fairytale- Tori Amos
Scars to your Beautiful- Alessia Cara
Rise- Katy Perry
Tangled Up in You- Staind
Flashlight- Jessie J
Uncover- Zara Larsson
I Was Made for Loving You- Tori Kelly
Masterpiece- Jessie J
Beauty and the Beast- Ariana Grande
Dear Agony- Breaking Benjamin

For a rose can wither in darkness, but burn in the light.

Chapter 1

Blinding chaos.

The car door opens, and a wall of paparazzi close in on us, fighting for a prime spot as they shove and shout out their questions.

The noise is jarring. The flashbulbs, even more so.

It never gets any easier.

I push my oversized sunglasses up the bridge of my nose, obscuring my eyes from the vultures. Luke takes my arm, dragging me through the crowd before I can mentally prepare myself.

We're fenced by security. There's nowhere to turn.

Everything is too loud and too fast, and I'm not certain when this became my life. It feels like it isn't even my life. It feels like I'm trapped in a dream, watching from afar as I go through the motions.

Luke pauses when we reach the stairs of the hotel.

He always does this. He likes to feel important. Standing high above everyone else when he looks down on them and answers their questions.

His left hand is still wrapped around my arm, his fingers digging into the pale flesh.

He holds up his other palm to the crowd, silencing them. I glare at him through the dark screen of my sunglasses. My cheeks are hot, and my hands are locked into fists.

I specifically told him no questions. Not today.

Not ever.

I don't want to do this anymore. I don't want to be here with their eyes on me. Cold, calculating. Tearing me apart.

Exhaustion settles into my bones, and any fight I may have had drowned under the weight of my heavy eyelids. I can't remember the last time I had a full night's sleep. I don't even know what city we're in right now.

They blur together.

I'm running on caffeine and avoidance. But I know it's short lived. The press isn't here for the tour. They won't be asking about the show or my upcoming albums.

The masses are hungry for answers. And I'm the injured fish in the middle of a shark tank.

"We'll take a few brief questions," Luke announces.

His face is smug and proud in a way only he can pull off. He's charming as ever, even while he capitalizes on my tragedy to squeeze out every last ounce of media attention he can garner from it.

Later tonight, when I bring it up again, he'll try to tell me this is what's best. That the media cares about me. That we're bringing attention to my father's case, which is the most important thing we can do.

He's always been good at spinning things in his favor. The absolute best.

Any PR is good PR, he says. And for the last six months, my name has been splashed across national headlines more times than I can count.

American Star singer Isabella Rossi set for upcoming world tour. The question remains... beauty or talent?

I've read them all.

The articles proclaiming that I won the show based on my looks alone. The outraged fan interviews and rumors that I slept with one of the judges. Pregnancy claims and unflattering photos printed in ink for all the world to see. But now they have something else to lynch me with.

Something I can't stomach.

Luke picks out a reporter from the crowd, and she speaks into her microphone.

"Is it true that you are canceling your world tour in light of the tragic events with your father, Isabella?"

I don't have to answer because Luke speaks for me. Always.

"That is completely false. The show will go on."

The show does go on when he wraps an arm around me in a display of support for the cameras.

"Isabella believes her father would want her to continue her life as normally as possible while the authorities handle the investigation."

Lies. Lies. Lies.

It's all that ever drips out of his mouth. He doesn't know what my father would want.

He couldn't possibly since I don't even know myself.

"Isabella!" a man in the back of the crowd yells. "Is it true that you were sent a video of your father's execution?"

My hands tremble, and my eyes seek out an exit. A gap in the crowd. A dark hole. Anything to get away.

Luke gestures for security to remove the man.

"Those rumors are completely false and unsubstantiated," he announces.

"I'm done," I tell him. "Stop this now."

His hand tightens around my arm in warning, locking me in place so that I don't make a scene.

"Just look at the cameras, baby," he whispers. "Show them how sad you are."

I stare at him, and I am empty.

I don't know how my life came to this. How any of this happened. It feels like a blur of events I can no longer recall.

All I ever wanted to do was sing. I wanted to create something. I wanted to be an artist. But somewhere along the way, art turned into marketing, and marketing turned into a puppet show with Luke controlling the strings.

That flame inside of me has burnt out.

And the truth is, I'm not sure I'll ever be able to light it again.

Chapter 2

Isabella

"Omigod, omigod, omigod," Megan squeals.

I rub my temples and wonder if I play dead if she'll leave me alone. I've been trapped in this hotel suite with her for three days.

She pinches my arm, and I hiss.

"Omigod," she says again. "Do you even realize who that is?"

She makes a wild gesture across the room, to the guy that Luke is currently schmoozing. It's another big shot producer I have no interest in meeting.

Megan fluffs her hair and glosses her lips beside me.

"How do I look?"

Truthfully, she looks worse than me.

She's lost a lot of weight since we left the show. Weight that she didn't really need to lose in the first place. And the way she's constantly sniffling and never eats tells me she's been doing a lot more than drinking every night at the parties.

While Luke has me on a low carb diet, Megan apparently is on an all coke diet.

"You look... great."

Another lie.

They come easily to me now too.

I just want to be alone.

Megan is over the top about literally everything. She's the Regina George to my Wednesday Addams. After the show, Luke snagged us both for his label. It seemed like the right choice at the time, but I quickly realized not everything that glitters is gold.

Megan trots off, and Luke flares his nostrils when she approaches.

She'll get a mouthful about it later, but right now I'm too tired to care. The conversation lasts for all of five minutes before Luke moves it to a more private setting and Megan returns to the sofa where I'm currently parked.

She plops down beside me with a dreamy expression on her face. She wants me to ask, but I don't.

"You can't say a word if I tell you," she says.

Her excitement is one hundred percent false. This is the same girl who used to ridicule me backstage for the way I dressed. The girl who referred to me as Goth Girl and spread a rumor about me practicing the occult. I'm also pretty sure she was the one behind some of the online terror campaigns during the show, but I don't have proof of that.

I trust Megan about as much as I'd trust a chunk of cheese in a mouse trap.

Pretending is exhausting. But I learned a long time ago to go along with it. In this business, it's better the enemy you know.

"Wouldn't dream of it," I assure her.

She peeks over her shoulder to see if we have an audience- probably wishing we did- and then leans in to whisper in my ear.

"Luke thinks he can get me in on a collab with Lana Cruz."

Even if I did believe it, I couldn't find the energy to care right now.

A smirk twists at Megan's lips, and she thinks I'm feeling jilted.

She doesn't know I don't feel anything at all anymore. My life is a series of robotic events. Travel, sleep, write, sing. Rinse and repeat.

"We have to go shopping," she insists.

I blink at her.

And the level of her ignorance- her coldness- shouldn't come as a shock to me anymore. But it really does.

My father is missing. Possibly dead. I haven't eaten a full meal in two months. I can barely manage to get out of bed or wash my hair.

And she wants me to go fucking shopping with her.

"Hey, Megan?"

"Yeah?" she perks up.
"Tell Luke I went to bed."

* * *

I hide in my room for the rest of the night and search google for any piece of news I can find.

There's nothing new. Nothing but speculation. Speculation I can't stomach to read.

So I call Art.

Art works for the same sector of the government that my father does.

What they actually do, I'll probably never know. As for their actual job titles, they are both contractors. Contractors who have worked with the CIA and NSA. But the rest, they don't disclose. Over the years, my father always told me it was better I didn't know.

That was his answer for everything.

I tried to believe that was true. I tried to trust that he knew what he was doing and I didn't have to worry. But now that he's gone- everything has changed.

There is literally nothing I can do but put my faith into the people he works for, hoping they will come through on their promises. Hoping that they weren't the ones to make him disappear in the first place.

Art has been acting as liaison during the investigation. Relaying information back to me although there's never any to give. He is probably sick of me by now, but if he is, he doesn't say so.

"Hey, kiddo," he says from the other line.

"Any news today?"

"If there were, you'd be the first person I'd call."

I don't really believe that. As much as I trust Art, I still feel like the agency is covering this up. They aren't telling me everything.

They aren't telling me anything.

The only thing I know for sure is that my father went missing during a job he was doing overseas. I don't even know what country he was in.

"Have you had a chance to speak with Javier Castillo?" I ask.

Art is quiet for a long pause.

Javi is another thing that I was never supposed to know about. And Art has already warned me once that I should never speak his name again. That I should pretend I never saw his file or that my father ever mentioned it, for my own safety.

But my safety doesn't matter anymore. Not when I'm stuck in this purgatory.

"I have spoken to him," Art answers quietly.

"And?"

"And you already know the answer, Isabella. He isn't going to meet with you. He doesn't speak to anybody. He doesn't even leave his home."

"He speaks to you," I argue.

"Through email," he sighs. "Hell, Isa, I've never even met the guy. The only one that I know who has is your father."

"But you know where he lives, right? Take me to him. Just let me ask for myself. Please..."

"You know I can't do that," he tells me.

I can no longer hide my frustration or the sharpness of my voice.

"Why?"

"Because. I don't know where he lives. Nobody does."

"Except for my father," I finish for him.

Again, I don't believe that.

Before I even heard the news about my father, someone came into our house and took everything from his office. His files. His computer. Everything.

They have to know something. And I know Javi is the answer. He's the only lead I have to go on. But not if I can't get to him.

"I'm sorry, Isabella," Art says. "I promise I'll call you if I hear anything. Anything at all."

"Okay."

My voice is numb.

I don't even know if he says goodbye.

The phone is still plastered against my ear long after the call ends. Until I fall back on the bed and stare up at the ceiling and think back on everything my father ever told me about the mysterious Javi.

The recluse who lives away from the rest of society. The child that he used to spend more time with than his own daughter.

I grew up hating him. Resenting him. Wondering what was so

special about him that called my father away so often.

I asked him once if I could meet him. And I'd never seen my father so serious as when he looked at me and shook his head.

Never, Isabella. You must never meet him.

He made it sound as though the boy was dangerous. As though he were a monster. But yet, he was always there with him.

Always.

The door to my room opens, and I curl into myself.

It's Luke.

And he's drunk.

That never bodes well for me.

He shuts the door behind him and comes to sit beside me on the bed, his fingers trailing over the naked skin of my ankle.

I pull away from him.

"What do you need, Luke?"

"Is that how you talk to me, baby?" he asks. "After everything I've done for you?"

Everything he's done for me.

He claims to care for me, but it's not the way I want or need. He's supposed to be my guiding light as an artist, but lately, it feels like he's driving me further and further into the darkness.

I'm locked into a contract I can't get out of, and he exploits that at every possible opportunity.

"You've had too much to drink, Luke," I tell him. "I think you should go to bed."

"I think you don't tell me what to do," he says.

The room is quiet, and my body is rigid. I hate when he's like this. I hate him more with every passing day.

"I care about you, Isa." He reaches out to touch me again. "I just want what's best for you. Let me comfort you. Let me be there for you."

He wants to comfort me alright.

With his cock.

I shrug him off again, and he gets pissed. He grabs my arm and squeezes.

"Don't be a tease."

"Leave me the hell alone," I tell him. "You don't get to talk to me like that."

He tries to climb on top of me. And this time, he's taking it too far.

I knee him in the balls, and he doubles over, coughing in pain when I shove him off of me. I bolt from the bed and out the door while he screams after me.

But he's too drunk to follow.

I make it down to the lobby and manage to flag down a cab.

I don't know where I'm going. I'm supposed to attend a party tomorrow. I'm supposed to do a lot of things that I really just don't give a fuck about anymore.

The cabbie asks me where I want to go.

"The bus station," I tell him. "Just take me to the bus station."

Chapter 3

Isabella

The house that once seemed quaint and homey now sits stagnant. Brown patches of grass stain the formerly pristine green of our lawn. Dirt gathers in corners and crevices, and dust visibly lines the window sills from the outside.

But on the front stairs, a flurry of crimson rose petals blows in with the breeze, settling against the door frame.

Always the withered roses.

I don't know where they come from. I only know when they arrived. The day of my father's disappearance, these rose petals greeted me at the door.

There is solace in the dead beauty of the dark crimson. I collect them and keep them in a box above my closet.

I don't know why.

I only know that somehow, they share in the pain of my grief. I hope they never stop coming. And I always wish they would.

I check the mail.

Three more letters wait for me there too. Always from a different city. Always anonymous.

The first is a charcoal drawing of a raven perched on a windowsill. The moon is eclipsed in the photo, and dark, ominous thunderheads line the sky above. A sliver of lightning pierces the center of the image, so real it looks as though it's split the paper in two.

The eery scene sends a chill up the back of my neck.

The photos are always somewhat abstract. A message that often leaves me bogged down in the onslaught of disordered emotions they evoke. The lines are exacted so precisely. The artistry is pleasing to my eye in a way I can't explain, except to say that I am drawn to the darkness of these photos.

I am drawn to everything he sends me, and I don't know why.

I open the next letter, and I am confronted with a recurring sense of déjà vu. It is the same beautiful scrawl, only this time, it is words.

The same words he always sends me- this stalker of mine.

Sing me a song, beauty.
With words only I can hear.

My fingers map over the lines while I try to understand. I haven't told Luke of these letters. I haven't told anyone.

I'm not entirely sure why.

Only that it feels private. And I have not yet decided whether they are dangerous or simply innocent flattery.

The third and final letter contains the lyrics of my first song.

I try to imagine the man behind these creations. The lost soul who wanders and listens to my music. He tells me to go back to my roots. He asks if my fingers miss the piano, or do I really prefer being a pop princess instead?

I know what he prefers.

His letters all surround my early works. Before Luke got his claws into me and decided it was better for me to appeal to a younger demographic with an 'edgier' sound.

The ink had barely dried on my contract when he started changing the rules of the game.

I was caught. Hook, line, and sinker. The only choice I had left was to adapt. It's on constant replay inside my head.

I'm a fraud.

A phony.

Everything about me is fake, right down to my smile and the new lyrics I sing.

They aren't my own. Those are private now. For my eyes only.

And this man doesn't need to remind me of the things I already know.

I fold up the letters and put them out of sight.

My phone won't stop ringing.

When I draw a bath and climb inside, I imagine a current sweeping me away. One that could pull me backward- when life was still real and possible.

Luke texts me incessantly. Threatening to drop me in one message while apologizing in the next. When that doesn't work, he reminds me that I'm under contract. He reminds me of the fines he knows I can't pay if I decide to stop being his puppet.

Inside of my chest, there is a gaping cavity where my heart used to be. And in the place of my lungs is lead.

I have to go back.

I know I have to go back.

And I will.

On Monday.

Chapter 4

She has come home.
Crying.
I replay the tape over and over. Observing carefully the way the droplets splash against her cheeks.
I like her tears.
My mouth waters when they spill down her throat and onto her naked breasts. She feels so sorry for herself, this little beauty.
She doesn't know the meaning of sorry yet.
My cock is uncomfortably hard and swollen when I retrieve the knife from my pocket. The flat edge presses into my thigh, and I imagine her cheek beneath my blade. I will see her tears again.
The tip of the blade digs into my flesh, and I twist until I am consumed by the pain. Crimson oozes from the wound, and I smear it over my bloody knuckles, shoving my hand into my briefs.
On the live feed, Bella steps from the bath, naked and wet with blotchy red skin from water that is too hot.
She does not reach for a towel. She does not move at all. Her eyes are on her reflection in the mirror.
Lifeless.
She does this often. Her lips are quiet, but I know her mind is loud.
She is picking herself apart the way the papers do. Wondering if she is beautiful, or if it is all an illusion. The overnight success with mediocre talent.

Some of the things they say about her are true.

She is beautiful. With pure, pale skin and ice blue eyes. Long raven hair that kisses the curve of her lower back. She is the most delicate thing I have ever seen, and she sings like an angel.

Mediocre, she could never be.

So clean and innocent and tender. The thoughts I have of her are so dark. The fixation blooms inside of me every time I watch her this way. She is a witch, and she has me under her spell.

This is not the way it should be.

She should be in my possession already. Every day that I wait, I risk losing my chance. I risk losing her to a force outside of my control.

An enemy of her father.

Anyone that ever knew Ray is being eliminated. One by one, I have watched them disappear in a series of car crashes and freak accidents. It's only a matter of time before they come for Bella too.

I need to move soon. Before time and circumstance have the pleasure of taking what can only be mine.

The light inside of her will be snuffed out, with certainty. But only by my hands. Mine alone.

And yet, something holds me back.

Something makes me question everything I have planned so meticulously. When I watch her this way, I have doubts. I need only to draw on my memories to vanquish those doubts.

Visions of torture fill my thoughts and my heart. The rage consumes everything good and leaves only bitterness in its wake.

That bitterness coats my tongue when I watch Bella crawl into her bed and reach for a book on the nightstand. So soft and carefree.

She has never known hardship. She has never known hate.

But she will.

Crossing her delicate ankles, she pulls her knees to her chest and tries to read. It doesn't last.

She is anxious. Fidgety. Distracted. And beneath her thin blue tee shirt, her nipples are hard. She discards her book and pulls the bed sheet up over her body. Frustration mounts when her hand slides down into her panties, into a place that I can't see.

She closes her eyes and breathes softly while she touches herself. My bloody fist chokes my cock while I watch. I punish myself for wanting her this way. For the thirst that breeds inside of me every time I see her pretty face.

She touches herself uncertainly, never quite satisfied. I imagine tasting her, and then I hate myself for it. I imagine her bound beneath me, immobile and under my control. Squirming, crying. Hating me and wanting me.

I want to hurt her. I want to mark her. I want to witness her blood contaminated with the blackness of mine.

Her phone rings, and it is Luke. She doesn't answer it.

Contempt surges inside of me, equal only to my viciousness. I want to rip his beating heart from his chest and force him to choke on it.

Isabella moans, soft and weak, and then releases herself with the tiniest of tremors in her body. Her eyes flicker open, and I zoom in on them.

I imagine my come dripping down her face and her throat. Marking her. Claiming her. Smearing my seed all over her body, mixing with the blood from my fingers.

The release is violent. My ears ring, and my lungs cease to function.

I am bloody and spent. But I wait until she is tucked into bed and her breath grows still before I move on to my next obsession.

I track his phone first. Luke is still at the hotel in the city. The bug planted in his phone allows me to hear everything he does. Every move he makes.

I take note of his transgressions. I take note of each and every one. And I bide my time.

He's fucking Megan again. High, again. He fucks her for thirty minutes and can't come. She asks if he wants another line and he tells her to piss off.

"Is this about Isabella?" she snarls.

There is a growl, followed by a soft whimpering noise. I envision him with his hand around her throat, threatening her.

"What did I tell you?"

"Don't say her name," she chokes out.

There's a sputtering cough, and then the sound of the door opening.

"Do you love her?" she asks.

There is a pause before he answers.

"So what if I do, kitten?" he taunts.

"Luke." Her voice is desperate.

"What does it matter?" he replies. "You're the one I fuck every night. Aren't you?"

Chapter 5

Art agrees to speak with me while I'm back in Virginia.

The house that I grew up in is about an hour outside of Fairfax, which is where Art requests to meet. It's at the same diner we've met at several times before, where the waitress knows him by name, and she doesn't make a stink about us holding up the table for hours at a time.

I spend the afternoon with him. He feeds me pieces of information from the investigation and tries to make them sound promising. They don't sound promising at all.

I still don't believe what he's telling me. Nevertheless, I continue to pursue my only hope. I plead with him to consider allowing me to contact Javi.

In the end, the result is the same.

I spend hours with him. Grilling him. Begging him. Wishing for any scrap of hope he could give me. It never comes. And eventually, he grows tired and unsympathetic.

He leaves me with the same line he always does. They will continue working on it.

The drive home is long and frustrating. I'm exhausted and I know I have to go back to Luke soon, but it's the last thing I want to think about right now.

When I turn the knob on the front door, it's unlocked. My palm hesitates on the handle, and I don't remember leaving it that way. I rationalize. I can barely remember what day of the week it is, let alone basic safety precautions.

But when I step inside, I know. I know something isn't right, even before I turn the corner and see the mess.

Someone has been in here. Someone has completely trashed the house in search of something. What, I don't know.

My first instinct is to call the police. But then I think of Art.

This could be important. This could have something to do with my father's disappearance.

I pull out the canister of pepper spray that I carry in my purse and walk through the house, checking to be sure whoever it is has gone.

When I'm certain that they are, I dial Art again. He answers with a sigh.

"Someone broke into the house," I tell him. "I think they were looking for something."

The other line is quiet for a minute, and then, "are you okay?"

"I'm fine. They aren't here anymore."

"You need to pack your things and leave, Isa. I will take care of it."

"Do you think this could have something to do with…"

"I don't know," he tells me. "I'm turning around now. I'll be there soon, but don't wait for me. Just pack your things and go back to the city."

"Okay."

"Let me know when you get there."

He hangs up, and I do what he says. I pack. But I can't leave like this. I can't leave without checking to be sure that some of my father's possessions are still alright.

There are things everywhere, strewn all over the floor. My books have been pulled from the shelves. The photos that remain on the wall are crooked, and the ones that aren't have shattered to the floor.

Even the photo of my father.

My hands shake as I pick up the pieces and replace them one by one. It's a long process. I save the broken knick-knacks on the floor until last. But when I move to sweep them up, something odd catches my eye.

And because of who my father was, I know exactly what it is before reality has time to sink in.

A listening device.

An icy draft crawls down my spine and settles into my shaking hands.

Someone has been listening to me.

Before I can even comprehend the full horror of my situation, I'm tearing the place apart. Searching the walls. Underneath the counters. The vents.

Things my father used to do.

By the time I have finished, it isn't only listening devices I have retrieved, but cameras too. The shockwaves have taken control of my entire body now. My heartbeat thrashes in my ears. My fingers tremble, and my lungs struggle to take in air.

It isn't the agency.

It can't be the agency.

Right?

But if not them, then who?

The cameras were in my bedroom. In my fucking bedroom. Where I changed. Where I... touched myself.

Oh god.

I think I'm going to be sick.

Chapter 6

Luke bought a plane ticket for this evening, but when I get to the airport, they tell me that I've been rescheduled to an earlier flight. I assume that it's also his doing. He probably thinks if I put it off any longer, I will lose the courage to go back. To smile for the cameras and pretend.

The flight is short. The ride to the hotel is short. Everything is happening too fast, and I'm right where I don't want to be again.

I feel sick. So, so sick.

I find myself wishing the power in the building would go out, and I'd get stuck in the elevator, just for the peace it would give me.

I'd welcome the blackness. I'd welcome it with open arms. But I have no such luck.

The elevator goes up without a hiccup. The keycard I had from before works without a hiccup. And everything in the hotel suite is as it was two days ago.

Only it's not.

Because this time I catch sight of Luke across the room, fucking Megan over the sofa.

His eyes are squeezed shut, and he's dripping with sweat. It isn't until the door falls back against my foot that they hear me.

Both of them freeze. Megan smiles. Luke looks horrified. And then angry.

He shoves Megan away.

He's already zipping up his pants and preparing to give chase as I flee to the elevator bank. I press the button frantically, but there isn't time. He's coming down the hall. So I make a run for the stairwell, but I don't reach it.

Luke snags me by the arm and whirls me around.

"It's nothing," he tells me. "Isabella, please. I don't even think of her. I only think of you."

I feel like I'm going to throw up.

"That doesn't make it better, Luke," I tell him. "I don't want to know what you think of. And I never want to see that again. It's disgusting."

"Disgusting?" he repeats. "Is someone jealous?"

God, the man is so conceited that's the only possible explanation that would make any sense to him. There is no arguing with him, so I get straight to the point.

"I want my own room. One where I'm the only person who has a key."

He laughs, and it's cold.

"Yeah sure thing, baby. How do you plan to pay for that? An IOU? It's a long wait until your check is cut."

"You're a pig."

He tries to drag me back down the hall, but I pull away from him and stand my ground.

"I'm not kidding, Luke. Either you give me my own room, or I go home. I don't care about the money anymore. You want to sue me? Go ahead. I'm not as stupid as you'd like to believe. There are ways out of this contract."

His jaw works and his eyes narrow as they fix on my face. I've never called his bluff before. But I really don't care anymore. He can bankrupt me. Ruin my life. Tell the media whatever he wants. I refuse to cave on this.

"You want a world tour?" I gesture back down the hall. "Then take Megan."

"Megan isn't the goddamned winner of American Star."

I cross my arms and refuse to budge. The tension is almost too much. But I can't do this anymore. I legitimately cannot take one more second in that room with the two of them, and I think Luke knows it.

He slides a hand through his hair and sighs. Then he turns on the charm. The same charm he used to get me into a contract with him in the first place.

"Fine, baby. Fine. I get it. You're pissed. You need to cool off. I understand. I fucked up, okay. I fucked up. I just… I want you so much."

"It's never going to happen, Luke."

My words roll right off him. He refuses to believe it.

"It will," he says. "Just give it time."

"Hotel room," I tell him. "I want it now."

"Okay." He holds up his hands in a gesture of surrender. "Just tell the front desk to charge it to my account."

I turn towards the elevators, and Luke takes a step towards me.

"Don't follow me, Luke," I warn him. "Not tonight."

For once, he listens.

I ride the elevator down to reception and check into a new room on a different floor under Luke's account. It is quiet and simple.

I lock the deadbolt behind me and turn the shower to scalding hot, stripping off my clothes before stepping into the spray. I stay there until it goes cold. Until my eyes are red and my skin is raw, and my feelings are numb.

I'm exhausted when I brush my hair and put on some face cream. I'm bare. Naked- emotionally and physically. I don't know how long I stand there staring at myself in the mirror. Hating the reflection of the person staring back at me. Wishing that girl never had any aspirations at all. Wondering if what they say about her is true. Wondering if her father is still alive. If anything will ever be good again.

I snag a pair of shorts and a tank top from my bag and pull them on before dragging myself to the bed.

I may not be able to count on the power in the building going out, but I welcome the blackness that sleep will provide.

Chapter 7

River bites into his apple and peers at me over the shiny red skin, chewing silently while he thinks loudly. He is seeking out signs of weakness in my eyes.

"Any word yet?" he asks.

"There is no need for pointless conversation," I tell him. "If I'd had any word, you would already know."

He shrugs. Takes another bite of his apple.

"Well, perhaps this is all by design then," he muses.

"What do you mean?"

"Perhaps there are more enemies in the woodwork."

"Again," I tell him. "This is something I've already considered."

"Yes." He leans back in the chair and props his foot up on his leg. "Perhaps there are many, in fact. We can never really know for sure, can we?"

He smirks, and I do not indulge him with a reaction. Psychological warfare is River's favorite leisure time activity. Usually, he can entertain himself for hours with subjects less intelligent than him. But that has never been the case with me.

"I'm going to move soon," I assure him.

He shrugs again. Finishes off his apple.

"I didn't even mention her."

"You didn't have to."

"Maybe you have nothing to worry about," he says. "Maybe they won't come after her."

"Your games don't work on me," I tell him.

But he is grinning because I am reacting as I told myself I wouldn't.

River reads me too well, sometimes. He knows I've been putting it off. But he doesn't know why, and he's made it his mission to get to the bottom of it.

"All I'm saying is that it seems you've moved on," he says. "It's like you don't even remember the cage. It's like you don't even remember the animal they turned you into."

One single word.

The cage is all I need to hear to bring back those visions. I close my eyes and recall the suffocating weight of death in my chest. Those memories flash through my mind in rapid succession.

The waterboarding. The torture. The hallucinogenic drugs and the interrogations. My body still bears the scars of those years. The years that I spent in the secret program made especially for children like me.

Children predisposed to murder.

I was exactly the target they sought out. When they took me from the asylum, it was a simple matter of what my file said. That I had killed my mother. The perfect subject.

I remember those words. Those were the last words I heard before they assigned me a number. A number that meant I was no longer part of the human race. A number that would become my only identifier in the darkest pit of hell. And when I had finally reached the end of my contract… when I was finally able to come home… vengeance could no longer be mine.

I open my eyes to meet River's. The resolve that wavered before is unhindered now. He smiles because he knows it too.

"Can you just imagine it though?" he asks. "The expression on his face when he learns of all the ways the student has surpassed the teacher?"

I can imagine it. I have imagined it many times.

"If you don't think you have it in you though, I'd be happy to volunteer," River offers. "I'm not as well-versed in torture, but I think I'd do a bang-up job of it."

"Like fuck you will," I growl. "You stay away from her."

River could do a good job of it. But the idea of him touching Isabella makes me want to murder my only friend in this world.

"You have plenty of willing subjects to play your games with," I tell him. "This one is mine."

He smiles again and leans forward on his elbows.

"Then what are you waiting for?" he asks. "Go and get her."

* * *

One night.

I will let her have the night.

I hate this fucking city. I hate Luke, and I hate this hotel. Anyone could get in here.

Anyone like me.

I stand over her bed and watch her sleep. The scent of lavender clouds the room, and this is how I know she is anxious. She always uses the oil when she's anxious.

There's a knife on her nightstand. Because she doesn't feel safe. She shouldn't.

There are so many predators out there. Predators like me. Predators like Luke. Even now, her phone vibrates from the nightstand with his name. Over and over. Never any peace. It has to stop.

I retrieve her phone and block his number.

Isabella flips over in the bed, and I freeze. It's not necessary. She isn't awake.

She is trapped in a tormented sleep, tangled up in the sheets. And now her breasts are visible beneath the sheer material of her tank top.

My hands ache to touch her. To feel her. I take the knife from her nightstand and trace the curve of her skin. She shivers, and it gets me hard.

I want to taste the blood that flows beneath her milky flesh. I want to feel it between my fingers, sliding over my cock. The tip stops just above her breast, and I force myself to drag it away, digging it into my thigh until it burns.

I must be patient. The rest will come. In due time. I know what I need to do.

The pain doesn't help. It doesn't keep me from picking up her journal and indulging in the obscenities of her mind. She writes these lyrics every day. Depraved and melancholy. They speak to me. They speak to me in a way that nothing else ever has.

It is a pipeline straight to the fucked up chambers of her deceptively innocent mind. These lyrics she writes are not lyrics at all, but only her own cravings coming out to play. Today's song is darker than the rest.

I am so hard I can't control my thoughts anymore. Her clothes are on the bathroom floor. And this isn't what I came here for. I tell myself to be patient. But I can't.

I find her panties, and I bring them to my face and inhale. Then I crumple them in my fist and unzip my jeans, wrapping them around my cock.

Isabella breathes in and out, and I watch her. Choking my dick violently with her underwear. Her skin is so pale against the Raven of her hair. So pure and milky and untouched.

I have watched her for so long. I have watched the way she turns up her nose at the boys who look at her. I have read the words in her journal.

The confessions of her raw desires.

She is a virgin.

An angel.

I've never had the opportunity to ruin something so beautiful before.

Her hair spills over her shoulders and skates across her nipples. Small and pink and hard against the thin fabric. I want them in my mouth. I want them on my face and on my cock. I want so much to feel her from the inside. To fuck her until I can't anymore.

This is neurosis. Fervent and miserable. The agony consumes me from the inside out.

I will destroy her. I will destroy everything divine left inside of her.

Coming on a choked sigh, I spill myself into her panties. I shove them in my pocket and keep them.

The man in me tells me to leave. The animal won't let me. I walk to her bed and sit down beside her. She is within arm's reach. But I won't allow myself to touch her.

Beautiful things must be admired from afar. Beautiful things must not be touched. That's what he always used to tell me.

He was wrong.

Chapter 8

When I wake, I am well rested. I felt at peace if only for a few hours. The room is still dim, but a familiar scent lingers.

A scent that feels like home. One that feels like comfort.

I roll over to retrieve my phone from the nightstand but stop short. The phone isn't there. Something else is though.

A solitary red rose.

So beautiful, so flawless, I almost don't believe it's real. At least until I bring the delicate petals to my face and breathe in the familiar scent of wild beauty.

And now I know for certain that I have not imagined it. The scent that always seems to surround me is not a figment of my imagination, and the rose petals at my house have not simply been carried there by the breeze.

Fear settles over me like a cold blanket as the stem falls from my fingers, the petals wilting to the floor.

If not the wind, then who?

I wrap my hands around the sheet and squeeze as my eyes dart around the shadowed room. I don't see anyone. I don't see a thing. But someone was here. In my room. And they left this rose right beside me.

The curtains are long and dark, and I'm too afraid of what might be hiding behind them. I'm too afraid of my own shadow right now to stay here another second.

I bolt for the door without grabbing anything. Not even a pair of shoes or my room key. Fear has taken the wheel now, and nothing is safe.

I have no idea where I'm going. What I'm doing. I just know that I need to leave. I need to get out of here. I punch the down button for the elevator repeatedly, but it's taking too long. My mind is wild with possibilities. And it keeps circling back to one thing.

Luke.

Did he do this? Has he been playing tricks on me all along? Is he watching me right now, savoring my fear?

I can't stand the wait. My heart is going to explode. My lungs are going to give out. Already, I can feel the air slipping away.

I bolt for the stairwell and run down three levels, listening for steps behind me.

They never come. They never come, and I am relieved. I can breathe again when I pass the second level. One more to go, and then I will be free. It is so close I can taste it. The fresh air. The escape.

I look back one last time as I fling open the heavy door. The door to freedom. But freedom is obstructed by a wall. The wall of a hard chest in front of me.

I was looking in the wrong direction. Because monsters don't always come from the darkness.

Sometimes, they hide in broad daylight.

Chapter 9

Before I even open my eyes, a vivid and familiar scent hits me. Wild roses.

I am surrounded by wild roses.

They are the first thing I notice when I come to. And they are everywhere. Crimson and soft velvet perched upon delicate stems riddled with thorns.

My eyes are dry and heavy, but a tear leaks from the corner and spills over onto my cheek. I don't want to accept my reality. I don't want to accept that this is anything more than a dream. But the high arched glass ceilings only confirm that I am trapped in a nightmare instead. A beautiful nightmare, with stars as far as the eye can see.

It's a conservatory. I'm in a conservatory. On a bed. Surrounded by roses and stars.

This is not a place I have ever been. And yet, it feels acquainted to me. A place from my memories.

My father used to speak of a place like this. A mansion in the forest. Moldavia, he said it was called. I didn't know where it was. At times, I often wondered if it even existed, the way he spoke of it.

But I recognize the architectural style. I recognize the trees outside the windows. They are things that I know can't be a coincidence. There is no doubt in my mind that I am at Moldavia. And the person who was leaving rose petals at my door all along was really Javi.

The same man who refused to meet with me.

The one I was so desperate to meet before.

I wonder now if Art knew. If he knew how dangerous Javi was and he was just trying to protect me. I can't understand it. Nothing about this makes sense.

Has it been Javi all along? Has he been the one who has watched my every move for...

I shudder to think of how long it's been.

That terror seeps into every one of my bones when I try to move and I can't. I am bound by my wrists to the bed frame.

My lungs burn with the need for air, and I can't think. I want to scream, but I am paralyzed.

Javi murdered his own mother. That's what his file said. And now he's going to murder me too. Tears well up in my eyes and I silently curse my father, wondering why he ever brought Javi into his life. Into our lives.

With a jolt, I ride the rollercoaster of emotions. Hatred. Anger. Paranoia. And then, finally, determination.

I'm struggling to pull free from my bonds when the sound of a door echoes through the cavernous space. A draft blankets the room before I ever see the shape of him.

Even then, it is all I can see.

He stalks around the perimeter like the predator he is, remaining shrouded in darkness. His hood is up, and his head is tilted down. A wildly overgrown beard is the only unobscured detail beneath the shadow of his cloak.

The magnitude of his frame increases as he draws near, veiled in jeans and motorcycle boots. Every step is a gunshot to my ears.

My breath has gone still, and my thoughts are careening out of control.

I need to convince him not to hurt me. I need to hurt him first. I need to escape.

He stops next to the bed, and those notions die a swift and brutal death.

A tank.

The man is a goddamn tank. And I'm going to die without mercy under the weight of those bear paws he calls hands. I don't stand a chance.

"Please," I beg him. "Please, Javi. You don't have to do this."

His name on my lips startles him, at least momentarily.

"You know of me?" his voice echoes through the space and sends another wave of terror straight through my chest.

Javi's file said that he doesn't speak to anyone. That's what Art told me. That's what my father told me. For all the agency knows- he can't speak verbally at all. But it isn't true.

It isn't true at all.

His words are accented with a Spanish lilt. Beautifully so.

And he said them to me. A low growl rises from his chest, and I try to curl into myself.

"How do you know of me?" he demands. "How do you know my name?"

"Your file," I whisper. "I read your file."

Another growl.

I squeeze my eyes shut, but it doesn't block it out. I can still hear him. He takes a step closer. Then another. And then he is sitting on the bed next to me.

When I open my eyes again, he reaches for me. His fingers touch my face. Rough. Huge.

Lethal.

I wait for his wrath. For my death. But it doesn't come.

His palm drifts down my cheek and over the sensitive flesh of my throat before dipping to my heaving chest. He's only an inch from my breast when he stops and jerks away.

The impact shifts his hood slightly, and I can see him now. See his wild, golden eyes staring back at me.

The scar that slashes right through his eyebrow. He has the bone structure of a Viking. One who looks as though at any moment, he might pillage my very soul.

"Javi," I whisper.

Again, his name on my lips seems to knock his senses astray.

He rises and disappears, only to return a moment later, placing a fresh cut rose on the pillow beside me.

"Why are you doing this?" I beg. "Please tell me."

"Are you ready, beauty?"

"Ready for what?"

He smiles. And his teeth are perfect. His lips, sinister.

"To sing me a song." He touches my arm with a feather light caress. "With words only I can hear."

* * *

When he releases me from my restraints, I dare to hope. I dare to believe that he isn't as bad as I've heard. That maybe there is still some humanity left in him.

A notion snuffed out completely in the next breath.

He reaches into his pocket and retrieves a red rubber ball with leather straps attached. When he moves towards my face, I try to jerk away, but he captures me by the hair and wrenches me back. My scalp burns from the force of his grip and my eyes water.

It doesn't feel real.

None of this feels real, and I just keep thinking it must be a bad dream. I will wake up and realize this is all some fucked up part of my imagination that conjured up this scenario. It's the only logic I can find in a situation where nothing else makes sense.

My father loved Javi. He treated him as his own son. And I can't imagine why he would ever want to hurt me.

Fighting him off is a fruitless endeavor. The man is a brick wall. More terrifying than I ever could have imagined. And the fact that he has something to hide beneath that hood only adds to the escalating fear in my mind.

He secures the band around my head and forces my mouth open to lodge the ball between my teeth. Once it is secure, he taps me on the lips.

"This will stay in place until I have a use for your mouth."

His words send another shot of adrenaline through my body, and it is pure instinct that has me trying to fight him off again. To flee.

I kick him in the stomach, and pain radiates up through the bottom of my leg as though I've kicked a rock. But still his grip on me loosens, and I grasp at the opportunity to run.

I make it ten steps before he's got me by the hair again. I try to scream, but it only vibrates against my lips. He turns me in his arms, and I cower beneath his shadow, waiting for him to lash out.

This must be it. I expect him to hit me. To kill me. I don't know what it is he wants from me, and I'm petrified to find out.

He reaches into his pocket again, and this time, he produces a knife. A strangled sound leaves my throat when he brings it to my chest and skims along my collar bone. I squeeze my eyes shut, and water leaks from the corners.

This can't be real.

It can't be real.

That's what I try to tell myself. But it is real. And this isn't how I want to die. I haven't even lived yet.

The tip of the blade digs into my skin, and I stop breathing. I think of my father. I wonder how he could have ever trusted this man. How he could have ever cared for him. And then I wonder if Javi is responsible for his disappearance.

The stark conclusion is a shock paddle to my heart.

My eyes open again and seek out the golden orbs beneath the hood. But he is skilled at hiding them. So much so that I can no longer even see the lines of his face. And the need inside of me is real. To know. To unmask him and see him for the monster he really is. The boy that my father trusted and cared for. The one he sacrificed his time with me for.

I hate him. I hate him with a level of passion I have never confronted before.

I try to tell him so, but the words don't come out the way they should. Instead, spit drips from the corner of my mouth, and my humiliation is real and painful.

But none of that matters. Because he is still wielding the knife against my skin. Edging the framework of my bones. And then he dips lower. So low, he's tracing over my nipples with the tip of the blade. They harden in response.

My body is betraying me. Disgusting me. Giving him mixed signals. I reach up and wipe the spit from my chin. And then I do something incredibly stupid.

I hurl it at his face.

Another low growl. And he tugs me closer yet. So close, I can feel the sickening hardness of his erection pressed against me.

This is turning him on.

He drags the knife between the top button of my shirt, slicing through the thread. I try to move, and he clutches me by the throat this time, with a palm that could crush the life out of me in one good squeeze.

I am completely powerless to him. The reality of that washes over me again with stark clarity.

I don't move. I don't even breathe.

I just stand there, frozen and numb while he slices through the remaining three buttons. He slices all the way down until only two halves remain.

Tears leak from my eyes when he does the same to the bra strap beneath. My breasts spring free, and he touches them with the knife. Dragging the blade over the soft mounds in an exercise that tests his own will. It occurs to me that this knife is the only thing keeping him from touching me himself.

And suddenly, I am grateful for the blade.

I don't understand it. I don't understand the darkness of his mind, but I realize that I need to. If I want to survive whatever fucked up game he's playing, I need to make sense of this. Of him.

He removes the scraps of my shirt and bra and allows them to fall to the floor. I squeeze my eyes shut again when he moves to my leggings and cuts through them too.

Nobody has ever seen me this way. Nobody has ever seen me bare. I feel raw. Exposed. Vulnerable. And there is nothing I can do.

The last and final piece to go is my panties. I try to beg him. I try to plead around the gag, but he doesn't listen or care. He slices through the silky material and rips them away too.

I am naked in front of him.

My body is consumed with fear, and I don't know what's going to happen next. I can barely feel my legs as he drags me from the room, a blur of wild roses and shadows.

The floor is cold beneath my feet, and I wish I'd grabbed my shoes. I wish I'd never left my hotel room. I wish I'd done so many things differently.

His strides are too large, and I can't keep up. My arm burns from his grip, and eventually, he grows impatient with me. Heaving me up like I am nothing more than a feather, he tosses me over his shoulders and clamps his forearm over the back of my thighs.

My head bobs over his shoulder, and my teeth gnash into the rubber ball with every forceful step. I try to count them. To distract myself. To focus on anything than whatever is about to happen.

He stops outside of an open door, and I stop moving too.

I'm gulping down breaths, and my heart feels like it's going to explode in my chest. I wiggle in his grip and have one last futile attempt at fighting back, kneeing him in the chest while my hands slap at his face.

It does me no good.

He simply grabs me by the throat again and applies pressure with his thumbs in warning. It is the smallest exertion for him. Barely any effort at all, and already, I can hardly breathe.

The resistance flees from my body in the presence of dread. I feel like a well-trained dog already. Bowing to his silent commands in such a short amount of time.

I fear for my sanity if this is only day one. Part of me questions whether it might be better if he did kill me now.

When he sets me down onto my feet, and my breath returns, it is the first opportunity that I have to take in the room around me.

It is simple. Barren. And also, horrifying. There is nothing more than a bucket in the corner. And a piano in the center.

A piano.

The thing that used to be my instrument of choice now terrifies me more than anything.

Javi makes a gesture to the shiny black nightmare.

"Play for me," he demands.

I glance up at him, and my reply is reflexive. Instant. A mumbled no. I wait for another threat. More terror. But it doesn't come.

"No?" he repeats. "Suit yourself, beauty. I will play you a song instead."

I don't understand what he means. Because he leaves the room, sliding the heavy door into place until the locking mechanism clicks behind him.

I swallow and look around me. At the nothingness. At the emptiness. I'm freezing, and there is no comfort to be found in here.

Not anywhere.

I wrap my arms around myself and walk the length of the room to keep warm. I'm hungry and thirsty, and I don't know how long it's been since I've eaten.

The hunger that has been absent since my father's disappearance is now back with a vengeance. My body is preparing for a fight. An all-out war.

But after a while, my feet are numb, and the walking isn't helping. My stomach is growling, and my eyes are heavy, and I can think of nothing else to do. So I sit down in a corner and curl into myself.

The floor is hard. Painful. Uncomfortable. But even so, the exhaustion from earlier events lulls me into a deep sleep quickly.

I don't know how long it lasts for. Only that I am jarred awake by the most horrifying of sounds.

Confusion and shock take me prisoner when I open my eyes and confront the images in front of me.

I never noticed it before. The projector on the wall. The projector that has now become my worst nightmare.

It's a replay of a well-known celebrity gossip show. And I am the unwitting guest star of their conversation. The topic is old hat.

Specifically, the rumors of me sleeping with one of the judges to win the show. Each host throws in their two cents before they read some of the twitter comments from the aftermath while they laugh.

Fat, talentless cow.

Her face looks like it got ran over and glued back together.

Bitch can't sing her ABCs. Go home, American Star, you're drunk.

Another waste of human space. Hope she gets hit by a bus.

The insults continue, flinging at me like arrows. It's a constant loop of interviews and my most caustic critics replayed at a volume I can't ignore.

I close my eyes and hum to try to block it out. I press my hands to my ears. It doesn't work.

I don't want to cry. I don't want to be weak. And I hate him for this. I have never met anyone so evil. Rage overcomes me.

I pound on the door until my nails break and my fingers swell. When that doesn't work, I launch my entire body against the frame.

I scream until my throat is raw. I force the ball gag from my mouth in a fit. And just when I think I can't take another second, everything goes silent again.

I stare up at the ceiling. At the blinking light where he is undoubtedly watching me from. I wait for the torture to begin all over again. But it doesn't.

Ten minutes pass.

Then twenty.

And thirty.

I curl up on the floor, on edge and exhausted. My eyes fall shut, and I start to drift off again. The moment I do, the projector screams back to life with more of the same.

This time, I do cry.

The tears fall and the words I can't avoid blister every corner of my mind. I don't know how long it goes on for. I can't tell night from day in this room. So I count the drinks instead.

Twice a day, he brings me a jug of water.

It isn't enough. And I'm never prepared. I never know when he's going to come.

So far, he's been six times. But I'm never fast enough to get to him. He opens the door without a sound and sets them inside. Then he leaves before I get a chance to attack.

He has to know. He has to know that I would kill him right now if I could.

I'm going insane. I haven't slept in three days, and I'm starving, and my mind is so fractured from this unspeakable torture that I could murder him with my bare hands if he let me near him.

I would try. And I wouldn't feel guilty for it. This is the animal he's turned me into.

In three short days.

By the fourth, I can take it no longer. The humming doesn't work. Talking to myself doesn't work. Blocking it out isn't an option. And so I do the only thing that I can. I sit down at the piano, and I close my eyes.

And I play.

My fingers are rusty and cold and numb, and it hurts. The pain is almost crippling as they move over the keys. But the sound that floods the room is such a welcome relief that I push through it.

I push through it until my movements are fluid and my voice is humming along with the notes. And just like that, everything else fades away.

My fear is gone, and I am playing again.

I think of the notes. The notes he used to write me. And his words.

*Sing me a song, with
words only I can hear.*

This is what he wanted all along.

When I open my eyes again, he's there. In the doorway. My fingers pause, and he shakes his head. The room is silent now. The projector turned off. And I've lost the will to fight.

This is my chance to kill him. To claw his eyes out. But I can't move.

I'm so tired. So numb. All I want to do is sleep.

"Keep playing," he tells me.

I stare at him. It would be so easy to give in. To do what he wants and stop this pain. This torture. But I can't bring myself to give up.

Not yet.

So, I stop playing.

He leaves the room again. The projector does not come on again. Not that night. Or any after.

Instead, I am entombed in silence. Silence so deafening, it is a different animal altogether. I start to imagine sounds that aren't real. I start to see shadows that I know aren't real. I feel like I'm going insane all over again, and I don't know which is worse.

The room is pitch black now. There is no light to be found in this prison. Twenty-four hours a day, I sit in darkness.

I talk to myself. I pick at my skin. Bugs crawl all over me. I hear him in the room with me, breathing. At some point, I hear a baby crying. When I seek out the source of the noise, it disappears entirely.

He brings me food, but I never know when. I can't see him. I crawl around the floor like a dog, seeking it out. Always the same thing, over and over again.

Peanut butter and jelly sandwiches.

I eat them and want for more. My stomach is so empty that it is caving in on me. Sometimes, I catch myself biting my lip just to taste the blood.

I am feral.

Wild.

An animal.

And this is what he wanted.

I cry. I wail. I mutilate myself on the walls, cutting and scratching my skin just to feel something different. I haven't showered since I've been here. I go to the bathroom in the bucket, like a heathen. I get my period and have no choice but to use some of my precious drinking water to clean myself with.

I am disgusting. Ashamed. Cold and lonely and tender in a way that I never thought was possible.

At some point, my mind fractures completely. I feel it happen.

I am broken.

And I am willing to do anything. Anything at all. Anything he says. Just to stop this madness. So with my last scraps of remaining energy, I crawl to the piano stool and pull myself from the floor. I sit down and will my fingers to move. They are stiff and painful and bloody.

But I play.

I play a song for him. With words only he can hear. I sing him a song I've never sung out loud. With lyrics from my journal. The one that the world has never seen or heard before. And soon, the door opens again. This time, there is light.

It hurts my eyes.

It's so beautiful, I cry because I can't bear to look at it. To believe it's real. But he's there. And I don't stop playing. I don't dare.

I play him three more songs before he halts me. He comes to sit beside me on the bench. And he does something that I don't expect. He pulls me into his arms and pets my cheek reverently. I burrow into his palm. Into his warmth and his touch and his scent, so comforting after so long in isolation. And I hate myself for it.

I want to die for feeling this way. For allowing him to break me. For turning me into this slave to human affection, even at the cost of reaping it from a monster.

He holds me. He soothes me. And it is so confusing. It feels like a trick from this man who has tortured me for so long.

He kisses my face. I am foul. But he doesn't care. His lips are soft, and they feel good. I will do anything to feel good.

I tell him so.

"Good girl," he answers. "You are learning, my Bella."

I nod into his chest like a puppet. And then I cry. He rubs my back. Then he carries me from the room. Back to the conservatory. To the bathroom nestled into the far corner.

He deposits me in the bathtub. The cold porcelain bites into my skin and penetrates my bones. But I don't even flinch this time. I've grown used to the cold. I've become one with the agony. And right now, the smallest of luxuries, even from him… feels like everything.

"Lay back, beauty," he directs me. "It's time to come clean."

Chapter 10

Javier

She lays back in the tub when I ask without protest.

And finally, the beauty is broken.

It took longer than I anticipated. She is stubborn. Strong.

Even now, when she looks up at me with misty eyes, it pains her to give in. To break down and need these things from me.

The monster.

The beast.

Her captor.

If I had any sympathy for the sweet girl, I would tell her she has no reason to be ashamed. It is a systematic destruction of the human psyche that anyone will succumb to, given the right amount of time and circumstances.

But I am not sympathetic to her plight, even as I wash her and she responds to my touch like a well-broken pet.

She is beautiful. Lovely. Even as messy and shattered and filthy as she is right now. But I won't allow that to make me forget. She will pay. She has to.

It is the only way.

And so I wash her, but I do not comfort her anymore. Comforts must be earned. And right now, she still has much work to do.

"Why are you doing this to me?" she whispers so meekly as I wash her hair.

"To see if you are stronger than their words," I tell her.

This is not the thing I should have said. But it is exactly the reason I chose the method that I did. And I must remember not to be so honest with her. Because now she looks at me differently.

She looks at me like I might care. Which I don't. And she must never think otherwise.

"Bella," I reply. "Do you remember what I said earlier about having a use for your mouth?"

She doesn't answer me, so I tug on the wet strands of her hair until she squeezes her eyes shut.

I do not like her this way. Acting so delicate. Her nipples are hard, and I am certain if I were to thrust my fingers between her legs, she would be wet for me.

Little liar.

"Perhaps I was wrong," I say. "Perhaps you need to spend some more time in your piano room."

"No!" she cries and curls into herself. "Please, Javi. I will do anything. Anything! Just don't send me back in there."

Tears streak down her face, and they make me hard.

"You will do anything, you say?"

Her shoulders fall in defeat, and she nods. Her answer is quiet. Sullen.

"Yes. Anything."

I want to play with her. I want to torture her some more.

"So, you will fuck me?"

She blinks up at me, and my words do not shock her as much as I had hoped.

My broken toy simply nods and gives me another meek yes from her dry lips. The angelic virgin, so easily offering up her virtue to a monster. She is ruining my fun, and she should not be so agreeable.

My methods have been too effective, it seems. Or perhaps I am just being too picky with her. This woman confuses me. And I need to stop thinking so much.

I squeeze her throat, and her eyes grow large as I remove the ball gag from my pocket and secure it around her mouth once more.

"Until I have a use for it." I rub my fingers over her bottom lip.

She does not cry again. Even as I dry her and touch her with my bare hands. She does not try to move away, or even tremble beneath my touch.

My cock is still hard, but now I am angry too.

When she is dry, I drag her along to the kitchen where my dinner waits in the oven.

"Get on your knees," I direct her.

She does as I ask without protest, the threat of the piano room still looming fresh in her mind when I remove the hot plate from the warming rack.

"Are you hungry, Bella?"

Her mouth waters and she does not need to answer verbally because the evidence is dripping down her chin.

She nods.

"If you want to eat, you need to earn it. Do you understand?"

There is the slightest flash of indignation in her eyes, which she snuffs out with a nod.

"Good girl," I answer, soothing her with false security.

My dick wants a reaction from her, and I am determined to get it.

"Now get down on your hands and knees."

She does as I ask, her eyes focused on the tile floor while she waits for her next instruction. I kneel down beside her, hot plate in my hand, searing my own skin. There is pleasure in the pain while I watch her this way.

So submissive. So broken. So degraded.

Her father would be so ashamed. Appalled. He will cry when he learns of the things I have done to his precious daughter.

"If you spill this, beauty, you go back to the piano room for two weeks. Do you understand?"

Again, her eyes shoot up to mine, terrified. Resistant. And determined. She really will do anything not to be alone. How confused she must be, to crave my company so.

I do not give her further warning. Instead, I set the hot plate onto the center of her back. And apart from a strangled noise in her throat, she does not move. Her body is rigid, her jaw taut. She is trying desperately to transcend the frayed nerves beneath her sensitive flesh.

I walk to the dining room table and sit down, gesturing for her.

"Come to me now, sweet Bella."

She crawls towards me. Slowly and carefully. Her pale blue eyes staring up at me like a beacon in the night. And she really is stronger than anyone gives her credit for. Because she does not spill. She does not cry. She does not move, even after I've retrieved the plate from her back.

I spoon some of the pasta and chew while she watches. Her mouth is still watering.

Hungry.

Starving.

And I told her I would reward her.

"Are you hungry?" I ask again.

She nods eagerly.

"Then do I have a use for your mouth?" I tap the ball gag.

It takes her a moment to understand what I want. Her face falls, but still, she nods. What a pliable little fuck toy she will be. I remove the gag and watch her as I continue to eat.

She is confused. Unsure. Awaiting more of my instructions. But she needs to know that it won't always be so clear.

"I thought I had a use for your mouth, beauty. Why are you just sitting there?"

She crawls beneath the table without further insistence and positions herself between my legs. My cock is so hard I will probably blow my load in the first five minutes. How long I have waited to have this from her. How much I have anticipated it.

She unzips my jeans with a trembling hand and reaches inside to retrieve my cock. I hear a small gasp from beneath the table when she sees it, and I smirk between mouthfuls of food.

It takes her a few moments to figure out where to put her hands, and I don't help her.

I try to keep my distance. I try to focus on eating instead of her. I want to look. To watch. And this is how I know I can't.

I shouldn't want these things with her. She is nothing more than a toy to be used. A doll to play with. I must remember this. Even when she takes her first lick, and my balls squeeze and contract with the need to fuck her throat raw.

It is too soft. Too hesitant. This isn't the way I like it. I let her get a feel for it before I start telling her so.

"Do better," I demand.

Her nails dig into the material of my jeans, and she draws me deeper. But still too shallow.

"I thought I had a use for your mouth, beauty. Do I need to go elsewhere and send you back to your room?"

She makes another sound and drinks me all the way in this time. It feels like heaven. And now, now she is doing what I like. My dick lurches inside of her mouth, and I catch myself looking down at her when I shouldn't be. Admiring the way her lashes look against her pale skin, and the way her silky black hair falls over her shoulders and tickles my balls. I imagine what it will feel like to have her lips on mine, hungry for me. And then heat flushes through my body.

These are not things I am supposed to think of. Confusion causes me to reach down and shove her face all the way onto my dick, choking her.

She coughs and sputters around me, drooling as I grip her hair and fuck her face like the toy she needs to be. I call her a filthy whore, and she does not flinch. She does not recoil or slow down but instead pulls me deeper.

It must be my imagination.

I tell her she needs to do better. That her only purpose now is to serve me and please me. I demand that she learn how to suck my cock and take me whenever I choose. I ask her if she can do these things, and she tries to nod. Then she murmurs yes around me, her voice vibrating against my dick. It sends me spinning out of control, and I pull away from the warmth of her mouth at the last moment to teach her one more lesson as I spill my come over her face and her lips.

I milk every last drop from my dick before I squeeze it back between her lips and tell her to clean me off.

She licks me clean.

Softly.

Gently.

Sweetly.

All while my come drips down her chin and her throat. When she is finished, she tries to wipe it away with her hand, and I stop her.

"No."

She looks up at me, used and filthy and mine.

"Let it dry."

The contempt flashes in her eyes again, but she only nods. And then a quiet question, spoken politely, the way a good girl should.

"May I have some food now?"

"When I have finished my dinner."

She nods and remains on the floor between my legs while I eat the rest of my meal. And when I am done, I keep my word to her.

This time.

I allow her to make herself a tin of soup from the cupboard. She does not protest, and she eats too quickly, burning her tongue in the process.

I watch her eat like a wild animal, my dried come still on her face. Her body naked and available to me for whatever I may wish. And I feel the undesirable urge to hold her. To kiss her. To reward her in another way and tell her how good she is.

But I do not.

Instead, I wait until she is finished. And then I lead her back to the conservatory. Binding her to the bed for the rest of the night.

Chapter 11

Isabella

When he comes for me the next morning, I am exhausted. And emotional. The fear of the piano room still lingers, but my hostility cannot be contained.

"You can't leave me tied up like this," I tell him. "I'm not an animal. This isn't right, Javi. You have to know this isn't right."

He looks at me, but I can't make him out from beneath the hood this time. It's pulled low over his eyes, and he has to tilt his head just to see out of it.

"Is that challenge I hear in your voice, Bella?"

Even though his voice is harsh, he sounds pleased. I don't understand it.

I did not imagine the accent during my breakdown. It is still there. His words are not disjointed. They are eloquent and musical. And I think that his file was wrong. I think he has been speaking for many years without a hitch. It is perfectly natural to him.

"What do you want from me?" I ask. "You need to tell me, Javi. I can't do what you want if I don't know what it is."

"This is not your concern," he says. "I will have what I want regardless, my Bella. You will stay here. And I will own you."

I swallow and try not to lose it completely. I need to be calm. Freaking out will get me nowhere right now. Because if I'm calm, then maybe he will let his guard down and I can run.

"For how long?" I press. "How long do you want me to stay, Javi?"

His reply takes longer this time. The drawn-out silence only makes my anxiety worse. His voice is too quiet when he speaks. And this is how I know he means it.

"Forever," he answers.

Forever.

The word ricochets around my skull, obliterating what little hope I had left.

I can't breathe.

He really is going to kill me. Except, he's untying me now. Gently.

He's so much bigger than me. There's no way I will make it past him. There's no way I can fight him off. He removes the bonds from my ankles and wrists and then allows me to sit up, gesturing to a tray next to the bed.

Breakfast. He brought me breakfast.

I want to cry. I want to plead with him. But he doesn't let me do either of those things.

"Would you like to eat today, sweet Bella?"

I want more than anything to eat everything on the tray. But I am not naïve enough to believe that it will come for free. Everything with Javi will come at a cost. To my self-respect. My dignity. My humanity. And there's a part of me that wants to pretend that there is still a fight left within. That I am stronger than him- at least mentally, and I can defeat him in that way.

But basic human needs are a motivation unlike any other. When you have gone without for so long, morals fall by the wayside. Everything else falls by the wayside.

"What do I need to do?" I ask.

He tilts his head down, giving me just a glimpse of his dark beard and a flash of gold eyes.

"Lay back," he tells me. "On the bed."

I do as he asks.

"Spread your legs."

This time I don't move. His voice grows harsher. Huskier.

"Spread your legs, Bella. Or I will spread them for you."

I spread my legs and hate myself a little more. I can feel his eyes all over me. Assaulting me in the most intimate way possible. Visually penetrating the place I have never allowed a man to see before.

I am humiliated. Ashamed. Degraded. And he is turned on, evident by his heavy breathing.

"Play with yourself, beauty," he says. "Show me how you like it."

Again, I hesitate.

A low rumble thunders from his throat. And his next words remind me that I have no choice.

"Or perhaps you would like to play some more games with me, instead?"

I reach between my legs and touch myself. It is robotic. Stiff. Awkward. My eyes are squeezed shut.

I jump when his fingers find my breast, skimming over my nipple. My body responds to him, and a storm of emotions festers inside of me. I try to swallow them back down.

This monster is the worst kind of evil.

The kind that doesn't feel like evil when he touches me. The kind that feels… good. And when his mouth captures the soft globe of flesh and he groans, I am wet for him. It is the worst kind of deception. The worst kind of betrayal from my own body.

There is the sound of a zipper, and I stop breathing. Waiting quietly for what comes next. I need to be mentally prepared. And I am not mentally prepared.

"Open your eyes," he demands.

I open my eyes. Slowly. Hesitantly. He is right there. Solid cock in hand, next to my face. Swollen and throbbing with his want for me. I try to force my legs shut again, to prevent him from seeing the lie between my thighs. The arousal I don't want or need.

I can't control it.

His fingers grip my thigh and pinch.

"Don't try to hide the truth," he tells me. "I can smell how much you want me."

I squeeze my eyes shut and shake my head.

"No."

"You will take me, Bella."

"No," I say again.

"You will take me," he repeats. "Or you will die."

I glance up at him, so close I can almost make out the lines of his face. His mouth. He is rigid. So, so rigid.

And I don't believe him.

Maybe I just don't want to. But I don't believe he will kill me. I sense the struggle within him. I just don't yet know what that struggle is.

He watches me study him... and he doesn't like it.

"Suck me like a good girl," he tells me. "Get me nice and wet."

I breathe out and do as he asks.

I draw him back into my mouth, sweeping over the velvet exterior of his heavy flesh. The salty taste of his arousal coats my lips and tongue.

He doesn't let me have control. The moment he's inside, his restraint is gone.

He cups my head and thrusts deep, hitting the back of my throat and choking me. I gag around him, and he grunts out his satisfaction when spit drips over the sides of my lips and down my chin.

"Yes, my Bella," he praises. "Good girl."

His approval eases my nerves and encourages me. I relax into him and let him use my mouth. But the better I do, the more tumultuous he becomes. With his pleasure comes his wrath.

The next words out of his mouth are not praise at all. He calls me a lazy slut and tells me to go harder.

I do.

He grunts and then asks if I think I'm too good to suck his dick. I tell him I'm not. He rubs his cock all over my face, smearing my spit along with it. He tells me I need to do better. Learn faster. Do as he asks. But all the while, he can't stop groaning. And I rise to every one of his challenges, meeting them with determination. Because I can hear the lies in his voice. How much he doesn't want to like it.

It chafes at him. And it gives me power.

He must know that I know. Because he shoves my face away, allowing his own hand to take over as he glares down at me from above, telling me I couldn't suck a dick if my life depended on it.

I open my mouth to argue, and he squeezes my face in his palm to shut me up.

"Play with yourself," he orders again.

But I already am. Nothing is happening. If he thinks I will come, he really is insane.

"That's right," he says, and his voice is cruel. "I forget that this beauty can't even do that right."

To prove his point, he touches me himself. Jacking himself off with one hand while he fingers me with the other.

I don't want to like it.

I try my best to stay numb. But my body is a war zone of pleasure and pain. Humiliation and want. My legs fall wider, and he praises me again before criticizing me in the next breath. He says I don't deserve to come.

But still, he fingers me. And still, I am wet. So wet for him- for this- that I can hear his fingers slapping against me.

He hears it too. And he likes it whether he can admit it to himself or not. Because his breath is guttural. Broken and agonized. His hand squeezes the life out of his cock, jerking so violently I am certain he is punishing himself too.

But I can't focus on any of it. Because molten heat is surging inside of me like a volcano.

I try to fight it off. To resist. To focus on anything else. But I can't. I fracture around his fingers with something between a sob and a wail. My eyes fall shut, and I succumb to the pleasure, my ears ringing and my vision dancing with flashes of light.

Javi comes too.

Releasing himself onto my breasts with a long, tortured growl. He empties his cock completely and then smears the evidence over my skin. Leaving it to dry like last time.

Marking me.

Claiming me.

And I think this is it. I am humiliated but sated. Hungry. Starving. Now I will get my food.

But when I open my eyes, the temperature in the room has plummeted. Javi is erratic. Enraged. There isn't time to question or predict his behavior. He flips me over and pins me down with the weight of his body, settling onto my lower thighs.

My adrenaline spikes and my muscles lock when he removes his belt from the loops of his jeans.

I try to wiggle away. His hand crashes down onto my ass cheek, searing a hot palm print into the flesh.

"Stop."

The command is simple. Deep. Terrifying. And I obey.

But then he grabs my foot, and the terror is real.

"I did what you asked. I did everything you asked."

"But you didn't please me."

It's a lie. And I know it's a lie. This isn't fair. I can't play the game when the rules keep changing. When he punishes me for doing exactly what he asked of me in the first place.

I try to tell him so. But the words get swallowed down my throat when he lashes the bottom of my foot with his belt. It is an agony unlike anything I've ever felt before.

It is raw. Scorched nerves. Fire and hell. He doesn't hold back when he does it again.

And again.

And again.

I try to scream, but nothing comes out of my mouth. I try to move, but he is too heavy, and his grip is unyielding. I try to beg him, but the words don't make sense. And I'm crying now.

A sniffling, inconsolable mess.

When I think it might be over, he starts in on the other foot. I am so certain that I am bleeding. Flayed wide open. But when he stops and climbs off me, my feet are bone dry.

I scurry as far away from him as I can. Huddling against the corner of the bed. I rock back and forth like a lunatic trying to comfort myself.

For two minutes, he stands there. Quiet. Watching me. Judging me.

I hate him so much. But then he comes to sit beside me, this tormentor of mine. And he becomes my solace too. Taking me in his arms and holding me. Rubbing my back and kissing my temple.

It is so much what I need that my mind can't comprehend this is the same man who just inflicted the pain. Because I am broken. All I can do is cling to the comfort.

Bleeding more of my sanity.

My pride.

My dignity.

He is stripping me bare with his methods. Destroying me piece by piece. And he makes no apologies for it. I am certain he feels no regret. His next words only prove me right.

"You are mine to play with, beauty," he says. "I can do whatever I want because you belong to me."

I sniffle and allow my hair to fall in a veil around my face, shielding my eyes from this monster who torments me so. But it does not help. He is not finished. He tips my chin upright and forces my gaze back to him.

"Now thank me," he demands. "Thank me for making you come."

I stare at him in disbelief. Horrified. The very idea is so disgusting to me all I want to do is spit in his face. And yet, the words come out of my mouth.

Proving only one thing.

My mind is a prisoner now too.

And I am merely a puppet.

Chapter 12

Isabella

I had hoped to find the conservatory lacking so that I could use the excuse to leave this room. To make a dash for freedom. But I was misguided by this thought because the conservatory has most of the things I would need to leave the room for.

Javi has thought of everything.

My own toiletries await me in the bathroom. I don't know how many of my most private moments he has watched from his cameras, but if I thought I could forget that for even a second, I was wrong. This is the cold, hard reminder.

Upon further exploration, I find a mini bar stocked with bottles of water. Water that I drink so greedily, I end up with a stomachache. But perhaps the greatest discovery is what I find at the far end of the conservatory. An entire library.

A library in the middle of paradise. And if it weren't also my prison, I might cry at the sheer beauty of this incredible sanctuary that Javi keeps hidden from the world.

I've never seen so many books in all my life. I've never seen such a grand home in all my life. The Victorian architecture, the plush furniture, the stained-glass windows and antique conversation pieces- they are all things that speak to me. Things I would have dreamed of one day having in my own home.

In the back of my mind, I wonder if this is intentional. If he wants me to love this beautiful room where he holds me captive. If it is a conspiracy or mere chance that when the sky falls at night, it casts a blue light over everything inside and the stars shine through

the ceiling to dance on the floor below.
Is it all by design?
It gives me hope, and yet it confuses me.
There is not even a remote possibility that Javi cares about how I feel. I can't make sense of his motivations. Why has he been watching me? What does he want me for? The mystery only becomes more muddled as my time goes on here. But it feels important. If I can understand what drives him, then I can find a way to get past it.
It's my only hope.
I must get to know the real Javi. The one that hides beneath the shadows and the hood and the wild beard.
And until then, I must bide my time.

* * *

Javi comes again at lunch to deliver a sandwich, and like my meals before, he tells me I must earn it. I don't have to ask him how because he came prepared. With a cup of dry rice.
He makes me kneel on the grains for twenty minutes before he allows me to eat. He watches me the entire time. Silent. Brooding. Cloaked in darkness and secrets.
I grit my teeth through the pain and wonder how he became this way. What happened to make him such a monster? I don't ask him, and he doesn't speak to me again, except to tell me I can eat before he leaves quickly after.
And so continues my life over the next week. I read all day, every day, and do little else.
After checking the bathroom for cameras and finding it empty, I take a few baths as well. When I've grown tired of reading and need something else to keep me busy, I request a notebook and pen from Javi. But what he delivers this evening has the blood draining from my face.
It's my journal. My already half full journal. He hands it to me and tries to leave. My voice stops him.
"Did you read this?"
His back is turned away from me, shoulders tense. He doesn't speak, and I know... I just know that he has.
"What is wrong with you?" I demand. "Do you even realize

how fucked up this is? You watching me on cameras and listening to me in my own home. Kidnapping me... and now this... reading my journal..."

I choke on the words, and strangely enough, that feels like the worst of his offenses. Because these words are private.

So very private.

So very shameful.

My face is hot even thinking about him exploring the darkest and most intimate corners of my mind.

"You had no right!" I yell at him. "Let me go."

He turns deliberately on his heel. Slow. Too slow. Deadly and massive. Looming over me like a black cloud. I back away, but there's nowhere for me to go. I'm pinned between him and the bed.

"I had no right?"

His voice is deceptively soft. And for a moment, I think that I am safe. That it's going to be okay. Until he reaches out and catches me by the chin, arresting my face in his unyielding hand.

"I have every right," he thunders. "You belong to me!"

My lungs fight for air when he drags me closer, the pulse in my neck beating a wild staccato against my delicate skin. Javi sees it. He sees everything. And he likes what he sees.

He likes to taste my fear.

But it isn't just fear anymore. It's something else too. A force of nature that can't be contained. It's a thrill. An adrenaline rush. A rollercoaster of want and need and hate and revulsion.

His breath whispers over my lips as he leans into my face. And I am not the only one at odds with my feelings. Javi is walking a razor's edge of control, his eyes swinging from destruction to obsession and back again. I never know which side of him will win. So I remain still and quiet, waiting for the storm to pass.

His fingers drift over my face. Soft and gentle and full of reverence. I don't understand.

What's more, I don't understand my response to him. He has conditioned me to accept his touch so freely. Not only do I accept it, but I find solace in it. Pleasure, even.

"I told you to be a good girl," he says. "I warned you."

"I'm sorry."

"Just one taste," Javi whispers to himself. "Just one."

He kisses me.

It shocks me back to life before I die all over again in his arms. I can't grasp what's happening. He's never kissed me before. And it feels so different. His lips are soft and warm until they aren't.

When my lips part, his tongue invades and conquers. He drinks me in. He nourishes his obsession. And he devours me. What started as a simple taste now feels like he is taking a part of my soul. His arms hold me prisoner so he can take from me what he wants.

He doesn't need to. Not anymore. Not when I am giving myself freely. Not when I am kissing him back. Drinking him in and nourishing my psychosis.

Without warning, he pulls away. Breathless, we stare at each other. Feverish cravings ignite the air between us. I thirst for him, still. And he hungers for me. But Javi can't and won't admit it.

The want in his eyes burns out, and malevolent storm clouds roll in. This is always the way with him. He reels me in and tosses me away.

I can't figure out what he wants from one minute to the next. Everything is a minefield, and I don't have the strength left to navigate.

I'm shaking my head already. Begging him not to do this. But my pleas fall on deaf ears. He drags me from the room. I dig my heels into the floor. I fight back this time. But it's futile.

He takes me to another part of the house. Cold and isolated. And in this room, there is nothing more than a wire cage.

I cling to his sweatshirt when he tries to push me away.

"Please, Javi. Please no. I will do anything. Anything you want. Please don't do this."

He smiles beneath the shadow of the hood, and his lips are cruel.

"Good, sweet Bella. Because this is what I want."

He shoves me into the cage- big enough for a dog- and engages the lock on the door before I can resist any further.

"Why are you doing this?" I ask through my tears. "Why? My father loved you! He did everything for you."

This is the wrong thing to say. And I never could have known the impact of this statement. I never could have known what it would provoke in him.

His fist shoots through the wire slot and wraps around my

throat without warning. And this time, it is not a game.

He is choking me. Watching the light dim from my eyes as I scratch at his hands. I think this is really it. This is how I will die. I never saw it coming. My hands fall limp at my sides, and I lose the will to fight. Only then does he release me. Rattling the cage with his fists and growling into my face.

I scamper back into the corner and curl into myself, unexpectedly grateful for the lock that separates us.

"He did everything for me?" he roars. "And this is why you are here, beauty. Because you are blind to the real monsters. The ones you've lived with all your life."

Tears track down my face as I shake my head in refusal. Denial.

"My father is a good man."

"Is?" Javi mocks. "How hopeful of you to believe his heart still beats."

"Was it you?" I accuse. "Did you kill him?"

He laughs, and it is callous.

"If I had killed him, Bella, you would know. For I would have delivered him back to you in pieces."

Now it is me who is unhinged. I grip the wire of the cage and rattle it as I scream into his face.

"I hate you!"

"Good," he replies. "That hatred will serve you well, my sweet. That hatred will be the only thing you have left when I am finished with you."

Chapter 13

Javier

Luke is looking for her. Making problems that I don't have the patience to deal with. So when I go to her today, it is with this simple request in mind.

I hand her the pen and paper and wait while she looks up at me. Half-timid, half curious. She should be afraid of me.

She should be terrified. So long as she fears me... so long as she knows I am a monster, then we will be alright. I won't lose control.

I won't forget.

"What is this?" she asks.

"A letter," I tell her. "To Luke. Tell him you are done. With all of it."

Her face pales, and her fingers tighten around the paper.

"You can't honestly think this is going to work," she says. "Javi, there are more people out there. More than just Luke will notice I've gone missing."

She's lying, and I know she's lying.

When I discovered that Ray had a daughter, I knew I had to see her. I had to know who she was. I had to know everything. And from the second I first glimpsed her, I have watched her.

She was only sixteen then. Ray was already leaving her home to fend for herself while he went out into the world to do evil.

It was foolish of him. He had so many enemies, and any one of them could have taken her. But they would not. I made sure of that.

Because from the moment I saw her face, I knew she would be mine. Mine to keep. Mine to play with.

I've watched her for so long. I know everything about her, and this includes who she keeps company with.

She is lonely. Surrounded by people, but still alone. Using her books to keep her company. Using her songs to make sense of the darkness inside of her head.

This has always been her way. She never fit in with the rest of society. She was never like them. She has always been an outsider.

Like me.

She only has Art now. Which she reminds me of in the next sentence.

"Art checks in with me weekly."

"I know."

She's quiet. And I am glad she does not try to lie to me again.

"If I do this," she says. "If I write this letter, will you let me out of the cage?"

"Do you not like it in here?"

She stares up at me, blank.

"Please, Javi."

Now it is me who is quiet because I do not know what to do. The answer should be simple. Always no. Never give her what she wants.

But she looks so lovely like this. Naked and filthy and mine. Her breath soft and her voice sweet and her nipples hard every time she sees me.

I want to reward her.

And it is a dangerous want to have. She is poisoning me. Making me forget.

"I just need something else to do," she says. "To keep me busy. Let me help you. Cooking and cleaning and doing the laundry. I can do those things."

She is trying to trick me. Just like he did. And now she does not look sweet. So perhaps I can be agreeable after all.

"You want out, sweet Bella?"

"Yes," she answers quickly.

"Then be honest about your father. About the kind of man he was. Tell me you are glad he is dead. Tell me that the world is a better place without him."

Her mouth falls open, and revulsion darkens her delicate features. It does not give me as much satisfaction as I had hoped.

"How could you say that to me?"

Her eyes are filled with tears now. When they drip down her cheeks, I want to fuck her.

She brushes them away and hides her face beneath a veil of hair, jabbing the pen into the notepad and scrawling across the paper in quick, angry motions.

When she is finished, she rips the letter away and thrusts it in my direction.

"There. You got what you wanted. Now leave me alone."

I want to punish her for speaking to me this way. I want to tie her up and flip her over and fuck her face down into the wire mesh of the cage.

But I don't.

Because it is better that she hates me. It is better that she understands what I am and never forgets.

Beautiful things were meant to be broken.

Chapter 14

Isabella

For the next two weeks, I bide my time. Watching Javi's every move. Seeking out a weak link in the chain.

I don't think there is one. He is regimental in the way he goes about his day. The times that he delivers my meals. The way he locks the door.

Every day is the same routine. He comes to the cage. He humiliates or punishes me with a variety of terror campaigns. Forcing me to spread my legs for him and play with myself. Sucking him off through the holes of the cage. Torturing my feet with his belt.

And then he feeds me through the cage too. Tossing me scraps like a dog before he leaves. He watches me. On camera and off. Of that, I have no doubt. Because there are cameras in here.

I spend my days writing and plotting my escape. It's the only thing I have to hold on to. Art has not come. Nobody has come. It was foolish of me to think that they would.

He checks in with me via text. Javi probably knows my speech patterns well by now. He could easily fool Art with his own replies.

Hope is abandoning me. I envision myself ten years from now, still locked inside this cage. But in this vision, I am nothing more than a skeleton. Because surely, Javi will tire of me by then. He will destroy what's left of me, as he promised.

Every day, the light inside of me dims.

And when I am finally certain that it has extinguished forever, something happens. Something that changes everything.

Javi comes to retrieve me from the cage. There is no explanation. No apology. No words. He simply leads me back through the house, along the same corridor in which we came. This time, he makes me walk.

My feet are bare, and the floor is cold, and Javi is not dragging me along by the arm. It gives me time to take in my surroundings. It gives me the opportunity to notice things I never have before. That's when I see them.

The trap doors in the floor.

I count three on the way back to the conservatory.

A renewed sense of determination blooms inside of me like Spring. When Javi turns to me, I wonder if he can see it. If I have given myself away.

"Tonight," he says.

"What?"

"Tonight, I have something I want from you."

I swallow and nod, playing the words on repeat in my mind. This is it. My chance.

Javi leads me into the bathroom and points to the tub.

"Wash up," he demands.

I don't want to.

I want him to leave so I can look for the door. But he doesn't. He stands there, and I go about the process of bathing, hardly noticing him at all as my mind considers the possibilities. When my hair is washed, and my skin is clean, he tells me to get out.

I do.

And then he is gone.

Leaving me to my thoughts. To my plan.

I am unnaturally still while I wait for the sound of the lock to engage on the door outside. I know Javi will deliver my lunch soon, which means I only have a short window of time.

The moment the lock slides into place, I dart out of the bathroom and begin searching the floor frantically. My heart beats erratically in my chest, and my fingers prickle with anticipation. But after three complete passes of the conservatory, I still have not found a door.

My eyes burn with unshed tears, and I can't accept it. I'm not willing to give up. I check every maladjusted tile. Beneath the columns of roses. The bookcases. And then, finally, the chairs.

I move them one by one. They are heavy and awkward, and I'm terrified that I'm making too much noise or that he could check the camera at any moment.

I have gone through them all. All but one.

The solitary chair that rests on a small area rug in the corner. It looks out of place there, and I have never noticed it before. But I notice it now.

My feet slap against the floor as I run towards it and yank the corner of the rug back.

I want to scream out my triumph. There is a trap door beneath.

The latch is secured with a small padlock, but the hinges are old and rusted. I glance up at the cameras, and for a split second, I am paralyzed. I never thought of what would come next. There are so many unknown variables with this plan. Javi could catch me. He could catch me, and this time, he would certainly kill me.

But I realize that it doesn't matter. I have no choice. I need to take this opportunity while I can.

My fingers scan the bookshelves for a hardcover. The hardest cover I can find. And though it is totally sacrilege, I use this as my tool of choice, striking the blunt edge against the lock.

On the third time, I have success.

I yank open the door and stare into the blackness, uncertain what waits for me below. It is dark and musty and old. I can't bring myself to move. I can't breathe. Fear threatens to steal my joy and keep me locked in place.

What if it's worse? What if I get lost, or...

I stop myself.

It doesn't matter. Nothing can be worse than what he's already done. I can only focus on one word right now.

Freedom.

I lower myself into the hole and shut the lid over me, obscuring myself in the blackness. The space is too small, too cramped, and it smells damp like the earth... and something more sinister that I can't identify. My hand moves along the passageway, guiding me.

I come to several crossroads throughout the path and use my best guess to find my direction. I don't know exactly which part of the house the conservatory is in. But if my sense of direction is correct, I believe it is in the East Wing which means I need to move west.

I move through the darkness for what feels like an eternity. It's taking too long. Javi will have discovered my empty room by now. He will be furious. And he will be looking for me.

The close confines are getting to me. I'm running now. Breathing too shallow. I trip and land on something hard and sharp. My knees burn, and the threat of tears is real, but when I look up, there is a tiny sliver of light peeking through another doorway.

I have no idea where I am beneath the house. It could be anywhere. It could be Javi's bedroom for all I know. But at this point, I have no choice but to chance it. I will get out of the house much faster than I will this passageway in the dark.

I push up on the door and meet no resistance. There is a small step ladder leaning against the wall, and I use it to climb up into the room. A room that looks like something straight out of a horror movie.

It is all tile. The color of light sea foam. It is cold and sterile, and in the center of the room is a surgical table with straps.

Straps stained with blood.

A wave of dizziness threatens to topple me over. Instinct tells me that this is the room. This is where it happened.

There is a drain in the floor beneath the table. A drain that is also stained with crimson.

I lock my knees, so they don't give out on me. I count to three and try to push through the nausea roiling around my stomach. My eyes move over the space, taking it all in.

The workbench on the opposite wall is filled with vials of different colored liquids. Morbid curiosity drives me to examine them. They are sedatives. Children's cough syrups. And in the pill bottles, prescriptions for Zara Castillo.

My legs feel like jelly as I continue my investigation. There are surgical tools scattered everywhere. Scalpels, forceps, scissors. Alcohol wipes and bandages.

I need to leave this room. I need to run away and forget whatever horrors happened here. But I am overwhelmed with questions.

Why did Javi kill his mother? Was he bad from the start? I have an insatiable need to know more. To understand him.

I can't explain it.

And I know that I am risking my only chance at freedom. But I also know I can't leave here without answers to these questions. I need to know what really happened to Zara. What horrors might await me if I don't escape.

On the wall, there is a projector. And beneath it, reels and reels of old tapes. It is a foolish thing for me to wonder what is on them. It is a foolish thing of me not to run as fast and far as I can.

I try to talk myself into leaving. But my eye is on the reel already in the projector. Just this one. I will see what's on this one tape, and then I will go.

I reach down and turn it on. It is old, but with a sputter, it comes to life, projecting the video onto the opposite wall. At first, what I see does not look like the horror movie I had imagined.

It is a woman. A woman that I recognize from the media headlines as Zara. And in her arms, a young boy. He must have only been eight or nine here. She is cradling him in her arms, singing to him. Encouraging him to drink the liquid while she hums a soothing melody.

He protests, but in the end, she wins by forcing the cup to his lips. After a time, he grows sleepy. When his body is limp, she moves him to the table and straps him down, kissing his hair and smoothing it away from his face.

"I'm going to remove the implants," she whispers. "I'm going to get them all this time, Javi. I won't let them control us."

On the screen, Zara retrieves a tray of surgical tools, and I swallow.

She sets them beside the table and lifts Javi's shirt. His body is so little here. The body of a child. And already, it is riddled with scars. Old and new. Deep and shallow. It is obvious that whatever this practice is between them, it has been happening already for some time.

As the film goes on, it becomes apparent that Zara was living in another dimension altogether. She proceeds to document her findings in a series of unintelligible words and gestures. Sometimes walking directly to the camera to speak, or alternately scribbling into a notepad.

A notepad already covered in black ink.

When she is done, she rattles off some information about Javi. His age and gender and a few other clinical details that seem to separate her from the reality of the situation, at least briefly. She sobs over him and then hits herself in the head, yanking on her own hair. Crying out that she doesn't want to do this. That she doesn't understand how they keep implanting him.

She berates herself for failing to protect him yet again. Then she whispers that they are listening. She must get the device out now. Her personality does another one-eighty when she reaches for a scalpel.

With the precision of a surgeon, the barbaric practice begins. She carves into Javi's arm, digging around in the flesh. When she does not find what she's looking for, her search continues on his leg. His abdomen. His chest.

And I can watch it no longer. I lunge for the machine and fumble with the buttons. On the screen, Javi is waking up. Crying. Bloody. Helpless. Pleading with his mother to stop.

I feel like I'm going to vomit.

And finally... finally... I find the power switch. The machine and the horrifying visions on the wall come to an abrupt end.

I'm still shaking when the door swings open, and I am faced with the adult version of the monster she created. His rage is a force of nature this time. Unstoppable.

Before he even comes for me, I know that I have crossed a line. This is a space I was never meant to see.

I am incapable of words when he stalks towards me and backs me into the corner. It is of little use to close my eyes. The monster is still there. He will always be there.

Javi grabs me by the throat and breathes into my face.

"If you wanted some pain, my Bella, all you had to do was say so."

His words are taken as they are meant to be. They terrify me.

I plead with him as he hoists me up over his shoulder and pins me down onto the same table he was tortured on. I apologize. I cry. I beg him and kick him and scream as he tightens the bloody straps around me and shoves my face down onto the cold steel.

He reaches for one of the tools on the tray beside us.

"Please, Javi. Please."

"Please what, beauty? Please remind you who you belong to?"

"No," I beg through my tears.

It doesn't matter. I know it doesn't matter. He tears open an alcohol swab and wipes the cold over my forearm.

I am afraid to move. Afraid to breathe. But still, I plead with him.

"I'm so sorry. I didn't mean to. Please, Javi. Please just let me go."

My words are swallowed back down my throat when the metal tip of a scalpel digs into my arm. The weight of his massive frame crushes me into the table. I can't move, but even if I could, I think I might be paralyzed.

The only sound in the room is his ragged breath. The knife slices into me again and I stop breathing altogether.

It burns.

But there isn't time to focus on the pain because it comes from a different direction each time he carves into my flesh. I don't know what it is. I don't know how deep the wounds are. But I can feel the blood dripping down onto the table. I can feel his excitement against me. His want and his need.

And my mind blocks it all out somehow.

The pain. The terror.

And when he is done, the only thing left are the endorphins flooding my system.

He dips his fingers into the blood and smears it over my cheek when he grabs my face and forces me to look.

"Mine," he snarls.

And that's exactly what his bloody artwork on my arm says.

He kisses me again. Brutal and demanding. I'm still trying to fight. Still confused. But the adrenaline surging through me is tainted by something else.

Something feral and toxic.

Javi tastes me like he owns me. Drinking from my lips and rolling his hips into me. He's feverish. Ravenous. And so drunk on me I am completely at his mercy.

He leaves my lips only to bury his face in my hair and inhale me. Whispering his secrets in Spanish. Touching me reverently in one moment and violently in the next. He licks the length of my jaw and bites down on my ear, sending a shock of pain and heat through my body. I buck against him and cry out, and he repeats the sentiment on my throat.

"Mine," he growls.

I don't know who he's trying to convince.

His hands are a hurricane, laying claim to the landscape of my body. My breasts, my back, my hips. He worships them all with his fingertips.

Warmth gathers in my belly and spreads down between my thighs. I can't help thinking of a similar scene. A scene that I wrote in my own journal. A journal he has read thoroughly.

His lips hover at the base of my neck, chest heaving. His fingers drag down my spine, and he follows. My cheeks are hot. Everything is hot. And he is too heavy. I don't know how to feel right now. I don't know what's right or wrong anymore.

The only thing I know is that when he assaults me with his mouth, I cry out for him. I encourage this fucked up need inside of me. Javi likes it. He likes it so much he tears the straps away and spreads my legs apart and shoves his face between them.

He licks me until I am raw. Until I feel like I'm going to explode. Until I hate him for doing this to me. I can't find the words to tell him so. Because he's possessed me. And I fear the only way to get him out now is to find an exorcist.

He unzips himself.

I plead with him to stop. To keep going. To put me out of my misery. It goes unanswered.

That's when I feel him against me. Scorching hot and rock solid. He rests his cock between the cheeks of my ass and grinds against me. Squeezing my flesh around him as he rocks back and forth.

I whimper, and he leans forward to suck the space behind my ear. His palm comes around the flesh of my throat, a reminder of his control. With a simple squeeze, he could end me.

I should be terrified. I think I might be. But there is another part of me- the part of me that wrote this scenario in my journal- that is unable to separate the reality from the fantasy.

He isn't supposed to know these things about me. These thoughts were private, and they were never meant to be real. He is violating me in the worst possible way. Infiltrating my mind and creating a reality of the depravities that live there. He is punishing me for exposing his own vulnerabilities. For seeing things that I was never meant to see.

"Javi," I plead.

He growls and unties my hand. The hand that is coated in my own blood. It is this hand he chooses to wrap my fingers around his cock. He is so large I can barely grasp him. So hot, it feels like he is branding my palm.

"Please," I murmur.

All the while my hand continues to stroke him. I'm tattered and torn. He is groaning above me. So deep. So masculine. So wild and untamed and desperate for my touch.

It's too much for him to handle. It's too much for me to handle. I'm ashamed and confused and turned on when I shouldn't be.

"Javi."

I keep saying his name. Over and over.

He yanks my hand away and forces both of them behind my back, pinning them beneath his wrist. His other hand comes up to capture a handful of my hair, wrenching my head back.

He is captive to his depravity now. Fucking the soft flesh of my ass without ever pushing inside of me. I can't see his face. I can only hear his sounds. Feel him against me. And still, it is the most intimate thing I've ever experienced.

"Javi."

He's moving harder. Faster. Rougher. I can barely breathe. My wrists are bruised already. Every part of my body is sore. But needy too.

I need something from him. Something I am afraid to admit.

Right now, he is only taking. Using my body to get himself off. And he is close. So close. I can feel it in the way his muscles tense.

When the tension finally snaps, he releases himself over my back with a long, tormented sigh. And then he rubs the come into my skin, spreading it over me in another show of ownership.

"Javi."

I'm pleading again. I want to tell him to leave. I want to beg him to stay. I want to see his face. I want to hide. His come soaked fingers move down between my thighs and over my sensitive flesh. My breath halts.

He smears my arousal with the blood on his fingers. And then he slips them inside of me. Feeling me from the inside.

He moves in and out of me slowly. Stroking the cheek of my ass and squeezing with his other palm. His breathing has calmed, and mine has not.

I'm squirming beneath him, my face buried against the steel table to muffle the sounds that escape me. My hedonistic desires are reflected in the noises that rip from my lungs.

I don't want him to hear.

I contract around him, and he grunts in satisfaction. I want to fight it. I want to prove a point. That he can't do this. He can't just take from me and do whatever he wants.

I also want to give in. I want to be completely at his mercy. Like my stories. Like my darkest fantasies.

In the end, it doesn't matter what I want. My body is a slave to its own cravings. And eventually, I come around him, just as he had intended.

It's embarrassingly wet.

Javi does not apologize. I don't expect him to. But I am not prepared for more of his cruelty either. He jerks me to my feet without warning and opens the trap door again.

"You want to play games, little Bella?"

"No."

My eyes are blurry, and my legs are still weak from the orgasm that just ripped through me. I can barely stand. I can barely breathe. But beneath Javi's release, his war still rages on. There is no escape for me.

He hoists me up again and drops me back into the hole that I came in from. And then he kneels down and pats me on the head.

"Run, run as fast as you can, beauty," he says. "Don't let me catch you."

Chapter 15

Javier

I try to stay away from her.
I try.
But she saw. She went into that room, and she saw. And now I want to punish her. I want to beat her ass red and then fuck it. I want to fuck her.
The virgin.
The innocent.
The beauty.
She was not made to be fucked by a beast like me. Beautiful things are not meant to be touched. But I have touched her, anyway.
How can I ever forget it now?
The softness of her skin. The catch in her breath. The way she looked face down while I debased her. The way I rubbed my come into her flesh.
My claim is carved into her arm. Her blood still coats my fingers.
A woman's body is the most sacred thing on earth. That's what River told me when he brought me my first. A prostitute. She wasn't soft like Isabella. But I fucked her nonetheless. She paid me weekly visits for two years. She let me do whatever I wanted to her.
Until I saw her. Until I saw my Bella. Young and faultless and pure as snow. My dick never wanted anyone else after that. But I had to keep it to myself.
Her father couldn't know the depravities that lay hidden within

my mind. The depravities I imagined with his own daughter. The most sacred thing on earth.

I kept those thoughts at bay. I told myself that I could never indulge them because he was the one. He was the one I would destroy. But he is gone now. There is nothing to stop me. Nothing to hold me back.

I want to take her. I want to make her mine. I try to tell myself I can't. That I won't.

But I know it's a lie.

It's always been a lie.

* * *

I smell her before I see her.

The scent of her arousal is still strong. Contaminated with fear and the copper of her blood.

Damp earth sinks beneath my feet as I follow her through the darkness.

She is trying to be quiet. But as I close in on her, she cannot hide the terror in her breaths. And I know when I touch her skin, her pulse will throb against my fingers. I will touch that dread in her veins. And then I will taste it on my lips.

I hunt her through the darkness, and her footsteps quicken. She knows I'm coming. She just doesn't know when or where.

She stops up ahead beneath a sliver of light, shoving desperately on a trap door that won't open. The light creates a kaleidoscope of her face, washing it in shattered splinters of orange and the salt of her tears.

Her hope is gone.

And I like her broken. I like her shattered. I want her tears. Her fears. I want the darkest and most intense parts of her. Every human emotion that she can feel, I will experience through her.

My steps are quiet, and she does not hear me coming. But my Bella is smart. Paranoid like her father. She can sense me. She looks down the dark passageway and freezes for a split second before she turns and runs again.

This time, I give chase.

Following behind her, I do not try to disguise the sounds of her predator. I want to feel her heart beneath mine when I capture her.

She catches her foot on a rock and cries out when she collapses onto her knees. Bloody and dirty and still trying to crawl away when she sees my shadow.

"Javi?" she whispers. "Is that you?"

The hope in her voice ignites the hunger in me. She wants it to be me. She dreads it being anyone else. And who else would it be?

This is a fear I did not know existed. One that I will exploit at a later time. But for now, I will take pleasure in this knowledge. And I will not answer her. Even when I catch her around the ankle and she screams, I give nothing away.

I lower the full weight of my body onto hers, pressing her into the dirt as I stroke her hair, and my lips find her throat. She shivers, and her heart is loud. Erratic. Beating so hard it vibrates up through her and into my chest.

She breathes in, and she is relieved.

"It is you."

My Bella is smarter than I give her credit for sometimes.

I flip her over beneath me and position myself between her legs.

"Please, Javi," she says. "I'm so sorry."

"Not yet," I reply. "But you will be."

Her chest heaves and she trembles when I grasp her throat and lick her face.

This has gone on long enough. I have been too kind to her. She has grown too attached to me. She should be afraid. Not relieved. And I don't know how this happened.

I squeeze her throat, cutting off her air while she claws at my wrist. I count the seconds in my head, quietly. And then I let her go, listening as she gasps for breath and sobs beneath me.

Now, there is fear. The way it should be. But when I reach down and touch her between her legs, she is still wet for me. Soaked for me. And there is something wrong with her too.

This sweet beauty is just as fucked in the head as I am, perhaps.

It makes my chest warm, and I want to kiss her. Hold her. These are not things I should want. So I unzip my jeans instead.

Her breath halts, and she clings to my biceps.

"Javi?"

I position the head of my cock against her wetness. Her

deranged need for me.

There is no more time for niceties. I plow through her virginity in one hard thrust. She bucks up against me and cries out, but still, she clings to me.

"Javi," she whispers again.

This time, I do kiss her. Because I have to. My own disturbed need for her is getting the best of me.

That voice inside of my head tells me I've claimed her. I own her now. She's mine. And nobody else will ever have her this way. Nobody else will ever get to touch her this way.

She kisses me back and digs her nails into my arms as I roll my hips and fuck her into the dirt. I tell her that she is nothing in one breath, and everything in the next.

She sobs and pulls me closer, burying her face between my neck and chest. Smelling me. Covering my skin with her tears.

I take one of my dirty hands and smear it over her face before I make her kiss me again. This time, she opens her mouth and lets me inside.

My cock is swollen. So sensitive I can no longer control my thrusts. I smash into her. Fucking her hard and fast. Pulling on her hair. Biting her throat. Sucking her skin until I taste more of her blood.

She reaches up. And tries to pull my hood down. I growl and capture her wrists, pinning them above her head.

"I want to see you," she pleads.

"What you want doesn't matter," I tell her.

I bite her nipple, and she cries out. In the next breath, I soothe it with my tongue.

I'm getting close. My body is alive. On edge. But it's her next words that trigger the explosion.

"I'm not on birth control," she cries out. "Javi, I'm not on birth control."

I bury my cock deep inside of her, and I come. I fill her up with all of my pent-up frustrations and the sadistic part of me wonders if it will happen the first time.

"I'm not on birth control," she repeats, and this time her voice is frantic. Terrified.

I stroke her hair. Her cheek. My dick softening inside of her.

"I know, pet."

She shivers.

"You want me... you want me to get pregnant?"

She is horrified. And I am getting hard all over again just thinking about it.

I think of her father. How much he would hate it. And I smile.

"It would be my greatest accomplishment, Bella."

Chapter 16

Javier

    She is reading when I bring her lunch. Feet curled up, bare against the velvet chair she likes. Her eyes rise to meet mine, and they are soft. Timid. Embarrassed.
    This is not the girl on TV. The one who they say is arrogant and stuck up and uses her good looks to get what she wants.
    This girl has never been any of those things. But she lets them think it. She lets them think she's that way. And I understand it all too well. I would tell her so, but she would not believe me.
    I set down the tray with her sandwich and move to leave. But she catches me around the arm.
    "Javi?"
    I glance down at her fingers, burning me even through the material of my hoodie. I want to know what her fingers would feel like on my scars. On my body. A place that I have not allowed anyone else to touch.
    When I look at her beautiful face, I know that I will never allow it to happen. She is tricking me with her looks and her soft words. When only hours ago, I took her virtue and fucked her in the dirt like the toy that she is. She should not be so agreeable with me now, and this is how I know she is a skilled liar.
    "I'm sorry," she whispers.
    Her voice is sad. And I don't believe it.
    "I shouldn't have gone into that room. I'm sorry."
    I move to leave. She doesn't let me.

"And now it's your turn to apologize."

I remain still and quiet, and her face changes from soft to hard.

"You can't just do whatever you want to me," she says. "That isn't how life works, Javi. I know you've been up here alone for so long. I know you don't understand normal social conventions, but even you must know the difference between right and wrong."

"You are mine," I tell her again.

She has always been mine. Since the moment I first saw her. Since the moment my obsession began.

"I'm not yours," she says. "I'm my own person. And what you're doing here is wrong."

"According to who?" I ask. "Who exactly says what I'm doing is wrong?"

"I do," she says, but her voice lacks conviction.

"Funny you did not say so when I was fucking you," I answer.

She is quiet, lost in her thoughts, fingers still wrapped around my arm. Small and delicate.

"I can't protect myself from you," she murmurs.

Her words anger me. And I can't stop myself. I lean down into her face, and she stops breathing. She stops moving. She trembles before me, and her fear makes me hard.

It makes me want to lose control.

"I did what you wanted," I tell her. "What you wrote."

Her mouth falls open, horrified. I squeeze her face in my palm and kiss her. Taste her. She squirms in my grasp and balls my sweatshirt in her fists.

She isn't pushing me away. Or pulling me closer. She is always so tormented about her feelings. The same holds true for me.

I pull away and stop myself.

"Eat your lunch," I demand. "And then write more."

She looks up at me, indignant.

"I'm not writing more. You never should have read that journal in the first place."

"You shouldn't have left it lying around then."

"You mean in the privacy of my own home?"

"Write more," I tell her again. "Or I'll write the story for you."

Chapter 17

Isabella

I estimate that I have been at Moldavia now for a little over three weeks. In that time, I have read more than I ever thought possible. Books upon books upon books.

Javi's library cannot be rivaled.

I don't think I could come close to putting a dent in it even if he did keep me locked here forever.

On my bad days, I wonder if I will ever be free again, or if it's true what he says. If I will remain forever in his garden of roses. If I will live and breathe and die here in this enchanting prison.

I write.

I write a lot.

And then I tear the pages out and hide them. Hide my darkest thoughts and fears and... wants... from the monster.

He must know. He must know that when he comes and reads the things in my notebook, they are not the only thing I have been writing. But he doesn't ask.

The story I'm writing now has captured his attention. He reads the new parts every day. Little by little. Chapter by chapter.

The story about the girl with the absent father. At first, the details of her life are mundane. But he reads them nonetheless. He reads how she goes to school and none of the other kids talk to her. So she sings, and she loses herself in the world of books. And then he reads the parts about her growing up. How her mother died when she was only a baby. She was lost without anyone to guide her, and her father was always too busy.

She decided it was a good idea to have several identity crises all before the age of eighteen. How her black clothing and nail polish prompted stares and whispers, but it also brought her peace.

She didn't want to fit in. She wanted more than anything to be different than them. To let them know that she wouldn't be stuck in that town forever. That she wouldn't be doing the things they all wanted to do. She wanted more.

She wanted time with her father. And she acted out to get it. But he never noticed. Even when she sabotaged her grades. He didn't notice. He was too busy.

With him.

The boy that he'd been spending so much time with. The boy that he seemed to care about more than his own daughter.

This is the part that Javi is reading today. He is enrapt as he scans over the journaled pages. His eyes are dark, barely discernible beneath the hood.

I wonder how it makes him feel when he reads about how she always hated the boy. How her jealousy got the best of her, and she resented him so much. But now she knows. She knows why her father spent so much time with him.

He felt sorry for him.

And now- against her better judgment- she does too.

He looks down at me. I want him to take off his hood. I want to see his face. I want to believe that the man who lurks beneath the shadows is still human. That there is still something to be salvaged inside of him.

Society has cast him out. Labeled him a murderer. Locked him away in a sanitarium as a child. I don't know if anyone has ever really helped him. I don't know if anyone besides my father has ever really tried to understand him. But I am trying now. By being honest with him about my feelings. By provoking something in him too. I need to understand him.

And I want to believe that if I help him... that if I do the thing that nobody else ever has... that maybe he will set me free one day. That maybe he can be more than just the monster society has created.

Maybe he can be a man, too.

"Javi?"

He is still silent. Lost in his own thoughts. I need something from him.

Anything.

But he doesn't give it to me. He hands me back the journal.

And walks away.

* * *

When the time for dinner passes, I start to worry. Maybe I pushed him too far. Maybe this was all a huge mistake.

I'm worried for nothing. Because tonight when Javi comes, something is different. He's quiet, like always. Locked up tight, like always. But something has shifted between us, and I can't quite understand what it is.

He sets my tray down on the table beside me. And the food is different too. I recognize the pasta from my favorite Italian restaurant in the city.

It occurs to me that he ordered this.

For me.

But I don't know why.

"How did you know?" I ask.

It's a stupid question, and I learned early on he doesn't answer stupid questions. Nothing has changed in that regard.

He's on the verge of leaving.

"Wait," I stop him.

He pauses. Lingers in place.

"Will you stay for a while?"

He thinks I'm tricking him again. I'm certain of it. It occurs to me that I might be. That I could and should be. But instead, my own mind is the one playing games. Tricking me into craving his company. His time and his attention.

He has not punished me since he took me that first time. He has not touched me again either. He has even given me clothes to wear. Like he doesn't want to look at me anymore. Like he doesn't want to see me.

I am lonely and afraid and confused, and I don't know what comes next. Something is brewing inside of him, and I'm afraid I won't like whatever it is. So I have to take these moments- these small kindnesses from him- while I can.

"Please?" I ask. "I am tired of eating alone. Will you have

dinner with me?"

The very real vulnerability in my voice does not faze him. Because he does leave. And I sigh.

I pull the tray closer and pick at my dinner when the door opens again. Javi stalks back into the room, and this time he is carrying another tray. With his own dinner.

I bounce my knee and try to keep my cool when he takes a seat opposite me and starts eating his food.

He eats like a caveman. It is too fast for him to possibly enjoy it, and he is done within minutes. Meanwhile, my plate is still almost full.

I don't want him to leave though. So I use the opportunity to ask him some questions in hopes that he will answer them.

"You have an accent," I observe. "Where are you from, Javi?"
"Chile."
"Chile?"

I don't know why this surprises me so much. But his accent is not watered down, and he has been here for so long.

"I like it," I tell him. "I like the way you talk."

It is not a lie.

He does not answer.

"Will you tell me about the roses?"

"Your father said they were your favorite."

I smile, if only a little. They were my favorite as a child. But I suppose now I'll never look at them the same way again.

Something so beautiful and yet... so dark.

I have always been drawn to dark things. Even now, my fingers trace over the petals that have fallen onto the table beside me.

The last time Javi spoke of my father, it was explosive. It would be foolish of me to bring it up again. But how could I not?

"Do you know what happened to him?" I ask. "To my father?"

My heart is subdued while I wait.

"I do not," Javi answers. "I do not know, Bella."

I believe him.

I don't know why, but I believe that he is not lying about this. His voice betrays the certain torment he feels about my father. They were close once. Like father and son. But something happened to fracture that love. Something fractured it so badly that it has turned to hate in Javi's heart.

I don't believe my father capable of hurting anyone. It isn't the man that I know him to be. To believe anything else would be a betrayal of the worst kind.

I am loyal to my father.

My love for my father is unconditional. Something that has been proven time after time over the years. But I still find myself sympathizing with Javi for whatever wrong was done to him. The only conclusion I can draw is that it must have been a misunderstanding. Because my father would never intentionally hurt Javi. He'd never intentionally hurt anyone.

This much I know to be true.

But I know Javi won't see it the same way. And I don't have the energy to travel down that path today. So I change the subject.

"Will you show me your face?"

I can't look at him when I ask.

"No."

His hands curl into fists at his sides, and I sense he is getting ready to leave again. Logic tells me I should be careful. I shouldn't push too much too soon. But I need to feel like we're making progress. At this rate, it could take years before we get anywhere.

"I've already seen you," I point out. "So what harm will come..."

He's out of his chair before I can finish the sentence. Hauling me up into his arms and squeezing my face in his hand.

"You want to see the beast?" he asks. "Is that it?"

"No."

I try to shake my head, but it doesn't move in his iron grip.

"I just want to see you, Javi. Please."

"You want to see me so you can hate me?"

"No."

My voice sounds less and less sure, and that isn't helping the situation right now.

Javi spins me around and pins my back against his chest, caging me in with his arms. He's impossible. I can't fight him. I can't fight him, and he knows it.

I wonder again if this is it. If he's going to choke me to death. I close my eyes and wait.

He drags his nose along my neck, breathing me in. I shiver, and something else invades the space between us.

Something potent.

Something intoxicating.

"I want you," he grunts.

I turn to cement in his arms, and yet he pulls me closer still. His cock wedged against my ass.

"Let me have you."

His lips find my throat. Soft. He kisses his way down the column of my neck and over my collarbone. My breathing is disjointed. Too loud. My body's response to him is not to be trusted.

Do I want this? Do I not? I can't figure it out anymore.

His hands slip beneath my shirt, squeezing my breasts as he groans into my ear.

"Let me see you," I plead.

It's the wrong thing to say.

Javi is tearing at my clothes now. Clothes that I probably won't get back. I am powerless to stop him. Powerless to do anything as he tosses me around like a rag doll.

The shirt falls to the ground below. My leggings too. The bra comes next. And then he's reaching for my panties. I do fight him this time. And in the chaos, I tumble onto the floor and scramble backward on all fours, trying to get away. Javi stalks after me like the predator he is. Too fast.

He's too fast.

He catches me around the ankle and then kneels down in front of me, shoving me onto my back as he yanks my panties free.

I kick at him, and it does nothing.

He grips the soft flesh behind my knees with each of his palms and thrusts my legs up, exposing me to him in the most indecent way possible.

"Javi, please..."

He buries his face between my thighs, and I forget. I forget everything.

I forget if we're fighting or not.

I forget how to breathe for a minute.

His beard tickles and scratches me. But it's his tongue. His tongue is inside of me. And my body doesn't care anymore. Nothing else exists outside of this moment. I've never felt so exposed. So raw. It's intimate, what he's doing to me. It's the most intimate thing a man can do to a woman.

Before him, I never let anybody touch me. I never let them get that close. And now- it isn't enough. I want more. I want everything. It dominates me.

Javi is rough. He is demanding. And he is hungry.

I jerk against him. I reach down and touch his hood. He pauses, and I beg him not to stop. But there is a moment when he looks up at me. A moment where… something else changes between us.

"Please," I beg him. "Let me see you."

He ignores me and turns back to his task. Eating me out. Devouring me. And I am a slave to the way that he makes me feel right now.

I am captivated by the monster between my thighs. It's getting me high. High on this. High on him. I feel myself falling. It's all going to come crashing down. I don't know what will happen when it's over. But I don't care. I ride it out. Soaking up everything he gives me. And when I come, it is nothing like the orgasms I have ever had before.

It consumes me.

Cripples me.

Blackens my vision and transports me to another world.

I'm in a different headspace. One far removed from the reality of my situation. Because Javi is bending me to his will. Making me a believer in his cause. He's infecting me with his disease of the mind. And I can't seem to stop it.

He crawls up my body and draws out his cock, rubbing it against my chest.

He's fucking my tits. Taking what he wants from me, the same way he always does. But even that isn't enough for him.

"Please me," he demands.

His cock prods the edge of my lips, and I open my mouth for him. I don't know why. I don't know anything. Except that a sick part of me wants this. A part of me wants him to keep defiling me this way.

The head of his cock glides over my tongue, salty. Soft and velvet. He groans and then shudders when I close my mouth around him.

I can't suck him in this position, not really. He's got me pinned. So he takes control. Moving his hips forward. Sliding in and out. The gentleness doesn't last.

When he grunts, he thrusts harder. Deeper. My eyes water and he cups my head to hold me in place. When I look up at him, I can see how untamed he is.

He really is like an animal. Wild. Caged for all these years. He doesn't know how to do anything halfway. He only knows how to take. How to fuck. How to use. And I've become his new favorite toy.

The sick part of me likes that. She likes getting used by him. Getting mouth fucked by him. And she's the only one in charge of my faculties at the moment.

I reach up and touch Javi's thighs. The muscles twitch beneath my fingers. He likes my hands on him. I wonder if he's ever let anyone touch him this way.

His thrusts grow frantic.

I am sloppy. There is nothing pretty about me right now. My mascara drips down my cheeks, joining the dribble from my mouth. Javi likes it. He likes me dirty like this.

I like me dirty like this too.

Unpretty.

His cock sinks into the back of my throat, and he comes with a violent shudder. I cough and swallow his release, my throat bobbing around him.

He pets my cheek and continues to rock forward, even as his cock softens in my mouth. I keep nursing him until he pulls away and zips himself up.

He lifts me into his arms, still naked, and carries me to the bed.

I am weak.

Used.

Confused.

I don't want him to leave. But that's exactly what he does.

Chapter 18

Javier

    She is soft this morning. Everything about her is soft. Relaxed. Her eyes are different today, lost in the pages of the book she reads.
    She is captivated. But peaceful too.
    She did not hear me come in. I like to watch her this way. It is different from the camera. I like to be close to her. In the same room where I can smell her. The room where I have tasted her. The room where I have held her captive for so long.
    I like the idea of keeping her in this room forever. Where she is safe. Where she is most lovely and delicate. But my Bella is not a rose, and she cannot grow in this room.
    Nothing else can grow in this room.
    Surrounded by such beauty, this room has opened her eyes to the monster that I am. It has served its purpose. And now it is time to move forward with my plan.
    She looks up, startled, and her fingers curl around the book. Her knuckles pale and rigid, her lips scarlet red.
    "Javi?"
    I don't have her breakfast, and she wonders what this could mean for her. What fresh new hell I might possibly have planned. My Bella is so smart.
    "Come, my sweet."
    She doesn't move.
    "What's going on?"
    "I want to show you something."

She does not give in easily. It happens gradually. Inch by inch, second by second. Until she finally sets her book aside and rises to her feet.

She is in a pretty dress today. Pale white and lace. And I wonder if she wore it for me. And then I wonder if I have forgotten who I am.

She steps beside me, so small and fragile. I worry that I will break her when I see her this way. When I see the size of her next to me. This is why I must control myself.

I walk towards the door to the conservatory, and she follows, hurrying along beside me. She takes three steps for my one, and I'm uncertain how to handle this, so I let her rush along beside me.

When we reach the door, I pause. She looks up at me. Nervous. Eyes filled with restrained hope.

"I am going to show you Moldavia," I tell her.

"Okay," she whispers.

"Do not try to run from me, Bella," I warn. "I should not have to remind you of the consequences of such an attempt."

She nods.

I don't know what she is thinking. If she plans to attempt escape.

I am uncertain. But I unlock the door anyway and leave her to follow me. She is quiet while we walk, her eyes soaking up everything around us. Her fingers reach out to brush the ornate details of each table and piece of art that we pass.

I show her the rooms without telling her what they are. Without speaking at all. I allow her to look through them, one by one. To become familiar.

I want her to feel at home here. I want her to experience these comforts and believe that she is safe. Secure. The way she feels right now.

It is exactly what I intended to do. But I did not expect it to be so easy on my part. Or that I would enjoy watching her luxuriate in the comfort. Watching each day pass as she reads and settles into her prison and her life here with me. Enjoying the food I bring her that she doesn't have to earn. Enjoying the clothing and gifts I bestow her.

It should not feel good to give her these things. It should not affect me at all. But it has. And now, I know that it is time. I must stop this from going any further. I must remind her who she is. And more importantly, who I am.

She is pleased with the house. She enjoys each room that I show her.Until I lead her to the one that she knows best.

It is well lit now. The bucket is long gone, and the floor clean. But it still possesses the same lingering effect. She stares at it, and her fingers tremble.

For a moment, I find myself wishing she would be stronger. That she would not be afraid, and she would simply sing a song for me. I miss hearing her voice.

"Play for me," I demand.

She blinks, startled, and then turns to me slowly.

"You can't be serious."

She tries to edge backward, but I take hold of her arm.

"This is what you do," I tell her. "You sing, and you play."

She turns up her chin and tries to look tougher than she feels right now.

"No."

This is exactly the response I wanted. The one I anticipated. And yet, I feel disappointed.

I know what I should say next. What I need to do next. But it does not happen the way it should.

"Why do you let it bother you?"

"What?" she asks.

"What they say about you?"

Her face is sharp now, all her softness gone. I do not like this.

"Why do you lock yourself up here and speak to nobody?" she challenges.

I don't reply, so she takes it upon herself to answer for me.

"Because of what they say about you. That you are a murderer. That you killed your own..."

I slam her against the wall and wrap my hand around her throat before I can stop myself. Before I can breathe. My temper is running hot, and she is not backing down this time.

"Did you do it?" she wheezes. "Did you kill her?"

I squeeze a little harder.

"Shut up."

"Will you do the same to me?"

There are tears in her eyes now. And this time, they do not make me hard. My fingers fall away from her throat.

We are both quiet. Breathing hard. I can hear the drum of her heart. See the vein pulsing in her neck. I can smell her fear. And her sadness too.

"Do not provoke me," I bite out. "I told you not to provoke me."

"It's not my fault you can't control your temper," she snaps.

Her lip trembles and one of the tears spills over her eyelid and down her cheek. I wipe it away with my thumb before I have given it any thought. She closes her eyes and leans into my touch. Eager for the brief moment of comfort I have provided her.

I want to do more. I want things that don't make sense. I want to hold her. Kiss her. Lay with her. It has to stop. It has to stop now.

I grab her by the arms and drag her down to the dining room. Her vulnerability flees in the presence of fresh terror.

"Javi?"

Her Javi is gone now, and only the monster remains.

I don't tell her so. I don't need to. She will see for herself. This temptress who thinks she can fool me.

I hoist her up onto the table, and she tries desperately to scramble away. She is fast this time, wiggling around as I bind her wrists to each leg of the table.

It occurs to me that I have spoiled her. I have let her get away with too much. I pull out my knife and slash the full length of the dress, halving it from top to bottom. Then I slap each of her tits hard until she calms down and obeys.

"Javi," she pleads through teary eyes and broken breaths. "Please…"

My only response is to bind her ankles next. So soft and slight and delicate. I pause only briefly to appreciate them, and then I snap myself out of it.

I remove the scraps of material from her body and toss them aside. Leaving her naked. Vulnerable.

Mine.

Just the way that I like her.

She looks so angelic when she cries, and I have forgotten how much I enjoy this. I was wrong to think anything had changed. That it could be any other way with her. Because this… this is what I need. What I want and what I will have.

I lean down to kiss her, and this time, the flames are back in her eyes. She bites my lip and makes me bleed. My lips smear the blood onto hers, forcing her to taste it. And then I pinch her nipples and make her cry out one last time.

"Tonight, beauty." I stroke her cheek. "Tonight, you will receive your punishment."

Chapter 19

Isabella

He leaves me for six hours before he comes back this time. I know because I count each chime from the bell on the clock.

I am cold. Dazed. Bitter. I don't understand him. I don't understand why he keeps doing this to me. Or what I've done to warrant this punishment.

When I see him again, I tell him as much. But he has grown cold again. Closed off again. Unsympathetic to my plight.

"I have to pee," I tell him.

He doesn't care. He forces my mouth open and reinserts the ball gag that I thought was long gone, tapping me on the lips.

"Until I have a use for it."

And then he moves down below me. Touching me. Groaning at the moisture he feels there. I try to mumble around the gag to tell him again, but it's no use. He can't understand, and my words don't matter, anyway. Not to him.

He pushes something inside of me, and it isn't his fingers. The resulting struggle I offer up is hindered by my restraints, and Javi just grabs me by the thighs to hold me in place.

"Stop," he commands. "Or you won't like what comes next. I'm being gentle with you. But that can change very quickly, Bella."

I don't understand what he means until he pulls the plug out of me and pushes it against something else. Somewhere he's never touched before.

I shake my head frantically, trying desperately to clench my legs together, but he slaps my thigh and makes me open for him.

"Be a good girl," he says. "And it won't be so bad."

The reality is that he's right. It doesn't matter what I do or how much I fight, it's going to happen either way. So I try to do as he says and relax.

He slips the plug inside of me, and it burns. It's too large, and my body is not accustomed to such an invasion. Not there.

I want to hate him. I want to scream at him. I want to rip off his hood and make him feel the way I do right now. Exposed and raw and wounded. But then he starts touching me.

Fingering me.

And my hatred is swallowed up by the intensity of these foreign feelings. The pleasure is amplified. Profound. It takes root in the nerves I never even knew existed and holds me hostage. My legs fall wider, exposing myself to him fully, and there isn't an ounce of shame left in me.

"You see, Bella?" he taunts. "This is the only way. You are mine. Mine to do with as I please."

It's a truth I can't deny. I am a slave to Javi. Always. To his touch. But it has never been so clear as it is right now. He owns me.

I squirm and twist and thrash against him, desperate for more. He has created this animal. Bent me to his will and turned me feral. And he is so proud of his little monster.

He bends forward and licks my face. Pinches my nipple. Clamps his hand over my mouth and nose. Always playing his games. Reminding me who is in control. As if I could ever forget.

My bladder is full, and there is so much pressure. I worry what will happen if I give in, but then I give up caring at all. I cry out and convulse like a demon from the onslaught of the orgasm. It is the most intense orgasm of my life, and yet it has barely touched on what I want or need right now.

I'm a mess. Physically and mentally.

Javi moves around the table, and I try to get his attention, mumbling around the gag.

"I have to pee," I tell him again.

He gropes my breast.

And then walks away.

* * *

I don't know how much longer I can hold it.

The pressure is too intense. And I know this is what he wants. He wants me to humiliate myself.

The silence is even worse. There is nothing else to focus on. Until there is.

The doorbell.

It shocks me back to life. The doorbell means someone else is here. And I'm out in the open. They only have to walk down the hall, and then Javi's darkness will be exposed.

Hope blooms inside of me. This could be it. This could be my chance. I crane my neck to try to see what's happening, but I can't. I'm too far away from the hallway.

A foreign voice echoes down the hall. I can't let this opportunity pass me by. Whatever it takes, I will do it. My screams come out muffled around the ball gag, so I shake my head back and forth until I'm able to spit it out.

"Help! Down here. Please, help me!"

There are footsteps. Two pairs. They are drawing closer. My heart is beating so fast it feels like it's going to explode.

This is it. My saving grace. Someone has come for me. Someone is here, and this nightmare is over.

Except when I see the man's face, I realize that it isn't. Because he takes one look at me, and he smiles before casually taking a bite of the apple in his hand.

"So this is her, huh?" he mumbles around the half-chewed fruit.

"Yes," Javi answers.

The stranger nods in approval, his eyes roaming over my naked body.

"Very nice. So when do I get to have a go?"

Javi will not look at me now, and I fear the worst.

"Please, no! No, Javi. You can't do this!"

A heart-wrenching sob explodes from my chest. I know Javi is cold. I know he can be cruel. But not like this. He can't do this to me.

He comes to the table and pets my cheek. The sickest part is that I lean into him. I cling to his warmth and the safe haven he provides while I try to appeal to any humanity left inside of him.

"I don't want him," I say. "I only want you. Please, Javi."

He glances back at the stranger and smiles. The stranger continues to eat his apple, unfazed.

I hope that Javi will ask him to leave. The person that I thought had come to save me is now scarier than the monster standing right before me.

"You want to please me, my sweet?" Javi asks.

"Yes. Anything you want. Please."

He unzips his pants. And the stranger steps closer. Watching as Javi shoves his cock into my mouth. My eyes remain glued to the intruder.

Frozen.

Unsure.

Javi slaps my breast to get my attention. I close my eyes and forget about the guest while Javi fucks my mouth and fingers me again.

I'm so wet for him. So sensitive. I have to pee so badly it hurts. I try to tell him. To mumble around him. But it's a lost cause. He's lost in his pleasure now. Using my face to get himself off.

His fingers tangle in my hair, and his eyes stake their claim over every part of my body. It does not matter what Javi says or what he does. Because in moments like these, it feels like he cares. It feels like I mean something to him, even as he uses me.

Perhaps it is only my imagination. Perhaps I am simply trying to justify. But it's there, and I want more than anything to believe in it. And when he comes, I swallow everything he has to give me, just the way he likes.

He pets my cheek again. And then replaces the gag I spit out earlier.

I think that it's over. I think that I've done well and that we have a connection right now, as he looks down at me, and I see the warmth creeping back into his eyes.

It doesn't last. I should know by now that it never does.

Javi retrieves a blindfold from his pocket and ties it over my face, obscuring my eyes.

My heartbeat slows. My stomach rolls. A chill creeps over me.

There are footsteps. The intruder. He's coming closer. So close he can touch me. I smell him, and he smells different to Javi.

I shake my head and thrash against the restraints, repeating the same thing over and over again.

No.

He wouldn't do this. Javi wouldn't allow anyone else to touch me. Because I'm his. That's what he says. But it isn't true.

I flinch when I feel fingers on my breast. Touching me. Groping me. My mind is playing tricks on me. But my ears aren't. It's Javi's voice that betrays me. Cold and hard and cruel.

"Now you can have a go."

I scream through the gag, and he moves away from me. Abandoning me. Footsteps echo down the hall. And with them, goes my fight.

The stranger drags his fingers down my body. Right between my legs. Humiliation and shame wash over me, followed by blinding hatred. I hate him so much.

I will never forgive him for this. Never.

I sob as the hands pry my legs open. And it doesn't feel right because this isn't Javi.

I want to believe it's a trick. I want my Javi. But he doesn't come for me. Not even when the stranger buries himself inside of me. The blindfold blocks the sight, but nothing else.

I can still feel him. I can still feel everything.

He fucks me. He touches the parts of my body that belong to Javi. He twists the plug inside of my ass. My bladder can't take it. I'm too full. There is too much happening. And I'm still too sensitive. I hate this man. I hate his hands on my body, his fingers working me over.

I feel sick for responding to him. It's not me. My body is betraying me too. Because I come again. And this time, the floodgates open.

Mortification burns my cheeks as the liquid drips down my thighs and over him. There is a muffled groan.

And then he's pulling the plug out of me. Replacing it with his cock.

I shake my head again, protesting as he pushes inside. The place that no man has ever been before. The place that even Javi has not been before. I beg him through muted sobs. I fight. I twist and thrash and bleed when the ropes chafe at my wrists.

Eventually, my chest caves in on me, and the only thing to come out of my lungs is a god-awful wheezing sound. It isn't the physical pain. This pain inside has crippled me. Javi has stolen everything from me. Right down to my last breath.

The weight of his malice has finally suffocated me. I can't breathe at all. I'm deep in the throes of a panic attack. And this is how I'm going to die.

My fingers make one last feeble attempt to claw at my throat. An instinctive reaction. One still hindered by the restraints. I fall limp. I stop moving. I stop fighting. The stranger's fingers come up to touch my face, and I turn away from him.

The gag slips out of my mouth. The blindfold falls away, and still, all I see is black.

My heart has lost the will to go on. My chest is full of cement.

"Bella. My sweet Bella. Shhh, it's okay now. Just breathe."

Javi.

My Javi. My cruel, cruel Javi.

I don't want to believe it. My mind has invented this. I squeeze my eyes to keep them shut, and he tries to coax them open with words so deceptively soft.

"It's okay, my Bella. Look at me."

He sounds so real. And I have to know. I open my eyes. Certain I will be forever damaged. Forever ruined and betrayed and filled with this hatred.

His beard is the first thing that I see. And then the hood. I look down, at the place where we are still connected. And it has been him, the entire time. Inside of me.

Tricking me.

Tormenting me.

I sob, and it is not pretty. He is without mercy. Without humanity. I was wrong to think there was ever anything else inside of him.

He leans forward and kisses me, his cock still throbbing in my ass. He tastes my tears and licks my throat. He comforts me with the sweetest lies.

"It is only me, Bella."

My breath has returned. And Javi does not waste this opportunity. He thrusts into me, groaning out his pleasure. And I don't understand this. I don't understand how I can be so broken. How I can be relieved that it is him, even after what he just did to me. He unties my wrists, and they are limp at my sides, but still, he drapes them over his back.

I claw into his sweatshirt, wishing I could draw blood, and he fucks me harder. Kissing me until I bite his lip again and force him away.

"I hate you!" I scream. "I hate you! I hate you! I hate you!"

He kisses me anyway. And he fucks me anyway. Telling me how good I feel. How much I please him. And then, how I am only his.

"Mine, Bella," he repeats with every thrust. "I would not share you. I never will."

And with these final words, he bottoms out inside of me and shudders out his release.

He collapses on top of me. Kissing my throat. Stroking my hair. Comforting me with his hands and his lies.

"I hate you," I tell him again.

But my voice lacks the conviction to make it believable, even to my own ears.

He unties me and carries me back to the conservatory. I am certain he will abandon me to my misery now. But instead, he climbs into the bed behind me and wraps his body around mine. Housing me with his arms and his warmth.

"My Bella," he whispers into the darkness. "Forgive me."

Chapter 20

Javier

In the quiet solace of night, her mind is still loud. Haunted by nightmares of the things I have done to her. The things I can't stop doing to her.

Even so, she clutches me like I am her savior. This girl has it so wrong. And I don't know how she still doesn't get it. That I am no savior. I am only a monster.

I swipe away her tears with my thumb, and she opens her eyes. Bluer than ever.

"You're still here," she croaks.

I shift away, and she squeezes her fist in my shirt. One by one, I peel her fingers off and abandon her to the warmth of the bed.

"I hate you," she says again.

But it is without heart this time. And when I look down at the hurt etched onto her sensitive face, I wonder if she will ever really hate me. If there is anything I can do that will make it so.

"Do you like the house?" I ask.

She lifts a delicate brow.

"You mean my prison?" she snaps. "Why wouldn't I love it here?"

"Then it is yours to do as you please," I tell her softly. "To feel at home."

"You're letting me out of the conservatory?"

She doesn't sound like she believes me.

"As long as you are a good girl."

This makes her happy again, and it is much better when she's happy. I tell myself so in one breath and hate myself in the next.

"The doors and windows are locked, so do not think about trying to leave."

Her face falls, but still, she nods.

"And you must promise to stay out of the West Wing."

"Why?"

"Just promise," I demand.

"Okay," she murmurs. "I will."

I let her get up, even though all I really want to do is kiss her.

"Come." I walk ahead and leave her to follow. "I will show you to your room."

Chapter 21

Isabella

Javi was not lying when he said that the doors and windows were locked. I know, because I have tried them all. Room by room.

They are heavy. Well built. And impossible to open without a key. He has thought of everything to keep me locked away in this gilded prison. That is the first thought that comes to mind. But upon further inspection, I realize that the locks themselves are actually quite old. They have been in this house for many years.

An artifact from Javi's childhood?

I know from the footage I saw that his mother was mentally ill. This offers a possible explanation. Perhaps I have not been the only prisoner within the walls of Moldavia. Perhaps... Javi was the first.

My father used to tell me a story when I was a girl. A story about a caged bird who longed for the outside world. For the wind beneath its wings and the fresh mountain air.

The bird would sing every day, yearning to break free from its golden cage. But little by little, the bird adapted to the cage. Over time, the enclosure began to feel safe. Slowly, the memories of the outside world faded away.

The bird could no longer recall what it was like to soar above the wind. It wondered if the memory was even real at times. And when the bird thought of flying again, fear replaced longing.

What if it could no longer fly? How could it ever feel free in a world with so many unknowns?

Now the bird had everything it could ever need.

Safety. Peace.

It spent its days singing and napping and snacking on seeds. Until one day when the cage door was left open by accident. The bird found itself powerless to leave the confines of the space.

It realized that it did not want to. The cage was home. What felt like a prison at first was now a sanctuary.

Whenever my father told me this story, I always felt so miserable for the bird. Every time, I would ask him for a different outcome. I would huddle beneath the covers, pleading that the bird would find freedom again.

But it never did.

My father told me that it was idealistic of me to ask for such an outcome. That life is not always so pretty. He said that sometimes the monsters lurking within us are worse than anything outside our safe spaces.

I never really understood those words. But here in Javi's home, they have become crystal clear. I get the analogy now. And I know what the bird represents.

Javi is afraid.

Afraid to leave Moldavia. Afraid to show anyone his true self.

He was imprisoned here too as a child. Taught to fear the outside world by his mother. And when she died, her predictions were only all too accurate.

Javi was taken away. Locked up. Abandoned with the rest of the bad apples. I don't want to feel sorry for him. How can anyone justify murdering a parent in cold blood?

I certainly never thought I could.

But my thoughts are shifting, the longer I am here. The longer I spend with Javi and come to understand his deep-rooted fears. He has been alone his entire life. Cast out from society. Taught fear and avoidance. Hurt by the one woman whose role it was to nurture him. The extent of which, I may never know.

Is it possible he snapped? That one day, he finally got tired of her hurting him? Is there a length of time that could ever justify his actions that day? What amount of pain must one endure before it is okay to make it stop?

I don't know. But I want to. I want to know everything about him. And that is a dangerous want to have. But once it takes shape in my heart, I can't stop it. I can't stop the sickness from growing inside of me. Day and night, it haunts me.

Javi told me not to go into the West Wing of the house. And this is how I know that is where my answers are.

It starts out small. I learn his schedule first. I observe which rooms he occupies the most. They are in close proximity to each other. All in the East Wing. Even his master suite is only two doors down from my room. But he has not come to me again. Not since he showed me the house that day two weeks ago.

He has left me to make my own meals. Meals consisting of what I find in the fridge and pantry. It is all child's food. Macaroni and cheese. Fruit snacks. Chicken nuggets. Hot dogs. And the makings for peanut butter and jelly sandwiches. I didn't realize it until now. These are the same things he's been feeding me the entire time I've been here.

He eats peanut butter and jelly sandwiches every day.

It occurs to me that Javi probably does not know how to cook. Because nobody ever taught him. I make a mental note of it. I make a mental note of everything. How long he spends in his office each day. Working on several computers. Doing what, I don't know.

Something for the agency. Something I probably don't even want to know.

At night, he goes to the room at the end of the hall. I would call it a gym, except it consists only of a punching bag and a weight bench. He works out like he's trying to kill himself. Then he showers. And he reads. This last one, I find surprising, though I'm not entirely sure why.

There are no televisions in the house. He doesn't listen to music. I suppose this is all he's ever had to do. Work, exercise, and read. He is a caged bird if ever there was one.

When I am confident I know his schedule, I decide that it's time to move forward. It is mid-week. After lunch. His office door is still closed, and I know he won't be coming out anytime soon. I also know that he can check his cameras at any time. But I can only hope that his avoidance of me has spilled over into the digital aspect too.

My journey is a slow one. This part of the house is dark. Quiet. Ominous. I stay near the wall and keep to the shadows, trailing my fingers over the wood paneling to guide my way.

The first room that I encounter is a bedroom. Another master suite. But this one belonged to a woman. Javi's mother. Her things are still here. Just the way she left them. Preserved beneath a thick layer of dust. Her blankets are turned down, nightgown draped over the end of the bed. Nothing looks out of place. It appears as though nothing has been touched since that last morning she woke up.

I move through the room like a ghost, afraid of any noise I might make. Afraid to even breathe.

It is her desk that has captured my attention. A desk stacked with journals. One by one, I leaf through them.

They are chronicled by time. The earliest are the works of the brilliant scientist she was known to be. But as the years progress, they catalog her descent into madness.

The later stacks are filled with gibberish. Words rewritten over words. The pages are almost entirely black in some of them, impossible to read. But the ones that I can see are clear enough.

She talks of the implants. Her fears for Javi. She speaks of the steps she needs to take to safeguard the house. Her shopping lists. Her projects. She details her suspicions of the mailman. The maid. Her co-workers. And gradually, one by one, she tars them all as spies.

It is when Javi is five years old that the surgeries begin. She describes them in horrific detail, right down to the precise muscles she believes the devices are implanted within.

She decides it is not safe to keep Javi in school and withdraws him. Shortly after, she loses her job, citing irreconcilable differences. There is an indication that the doctors are trying to poison her with pills. Pills she refuses to take. And the journal entries continue over the span of Javi's brief childhood.

Until the very last day.

Only one entry was penned on that day. Haunting last words.

They got to her too.

She can feel the device inside of her.

And it has to come out.

Chapter 22

Isabella

My exploration of the West Wing is a measured task. It is done slowly, day after day. I don't want to arouse Javi's suspicions, and there is only a limited window of time that I feel confident in my routine.

He continues to avoid me, for reasons I don't know. But if the past is any indication that could turn on a dime.

I question if he's even capable of feeling guilt for the things he's done. And then I wonder if he has tired of me. It shouldn't matter to me. I should be relieved. But instead, I am lonely. More isolated with every passing day. And I am hesitant to acknowledge that I miss his company. His warmth... and on the rare occasion he offers it, his affection.

Today, I pass by the remaining bedrooms in the West Wing. They are empty. Nothing to see. But I do find the surgery room again. And the tapes again. There are piles beside the projector.

I don't think I can stomach to watch any more of them. So I dig through the cupboards instead. Checking the labels and seeking out anything else that I might have missed before.

There are too many bottles to count. More surgical tools than most operating theaters probably have. Additional journals with irrational entries.

And one odd looking key.

At first, I dismiss it. Until I realize that it could be important. The lock on the door to this room is broken, and the key doesn't fit.

There is no window, so I go to another room and try the door and window there.

Still no luck.

I stare at it for a long while, trying to figure out what it could be for. As much as I want to believe it, it wouldn't make sense for Javi to have a key of importance haplessly lying around like this. He is too careful for that. Even if he forbade me from coming into this wing, he had to know I might still try. So I go back to the surgery room and poke around the cabinets for a clue. They are all unlocked. But they aren't attached to the wall. It is simply a standing row of shelves. Shelves that might have something behind them.

It's a long shot. And probably too risky to be moving furniture. Can Javi hear me in this part of the house? It feels so far away from his office.

I'm not certain.

Until I think of the bird again. And I realize that I am choosing safety over freedom. That if I really want to know the answers to my questions, I need to figure out what this key is for.

I test the cabinets by wiggling them with my hand. They are old. Rickety. But they aren't as heavy as I thought.

I start out small. Sliding them just an inch forward.

Pausing.

Waiting.

Holding my breath.

Javi does not come. So after a minute, I move it another inch. And then another. And after I've cleared about half a foot, I can see it.

The square shaped door in the wall. A built-in cupboard. With a lock. My heart beats faster.Louder. I move the cabinets again, not stopping this time until I can reach the lock. My arm almost gets stuck in my panic to test out the key. But with a twist, I hit gold.

The lock turns. The door opens. And my shoulders fall when I see the contents.

Tapes.

They are simply more tapes. But why are they in here? Hidden away. It doesn't make sense.

Down the hall, a door slams and jolts me from my thoughts. He's coming. He must know, and he's coming.

Gathering the tapes into my arms, I shove them into my pockets. I lock the door and slide the cupboards back into place. Footsteps echo down the hall, and I know I am caught.

He will be here any moment. And there is only one thing for me to do. I climb back down into the underground tunnel and run. Testing each latch that I come to with a sliver of light above.

I pass up five before I find one that is unlocked. Oddly enough, it is the same one I escaped into before. In the conservatory. I swore Javi locked it again. But it doesn't matter. He's looking for me. And I need to hide these tapes and find a way to avoid his wrath.

I dart into the one place in this room where I know he doesn't have cameras and shove the tapes into a makeup case before securing them in the drawer.

There is a loud crash from somewhere on the opposite side of the house. I don't know what to do now. How to explain my absence, or if he knows. I creep back towards my room but stop when I pass the piano room.

The piano.

I haven't played since those early first weeks. I haven't wanted to play since long before I left Luke when he tried to turn me into a pop princess. But Javi asked me to play. He wanted to hear me play.

And I can only hope that it will calm him now.

I sit down on the bench and take a deep breath, closing my eyes as my fingers hover over the keys. Feeling them. Reacquainting myself with them.

I don't open my eyes. But I play. The song that I had stuck in my head for so long, but was afraid to give voice to.

It's rough at first. I have always done better thinking of the lyrics as I go along. Finding the right notes. I play it over and over again until I feel like I have it right.

Everything else slips away. I forget why I came here as I get lost in the music. Nothing else matters at this moment. Not until I open my eyes and see him standing there. Watching me. Enrapt. Suspicious. I stop, and our eyes lock.

"Keep playing," he says.

I keep playing.

Javi doesn't say another word. He just listens. Watches. Waits until the song is over.

And then he leaves again.

Chapter 23

Javier

I have underestimated Luke. Underestimated his level of obsession, and also his reach.

He has hired a team of private investigators. He is relentless in his pursuit of my Bella. He is sniffing around too much. Making too much noise. Her face is plastered over every major news outlet.

Pop princess gone missing?

Rumors of nervous breakdowns abound. Fans theorizing a possible connection to her father's disappearance. Questions. Questions that I can't have. The agency can't know she is with me. And so it is time for me to quash the problem.

River arrives at seven, two hours later than he said he would. We give each other a brief nod, and then he asks me where the girl is.

If there is anyone I trust, it's River. We were in the sanitarium together as children. I did not speak, and he spoke too much. And as luck would have it, he ended up being my roommate.

He was annoying. Psychotic. But mellow, most of the time. And mellow was what I needed. When I wouldn't speak to him, he started writing me notes. In code. My brain liked the challenge. It took me a week to figure it out. He was smart, like me. So we wrote to each other. In code.

I didn't tell him my secrets, and he didn't tell me his. We just talked. About stupid things. But it was nice to talk about stupid things. When everyone else looked at me like I was the worst of humanity. Like I was a monster. River never did.

He was my first friend. My only friend. And he is the only person I would trust to look after my Bella.

I have no need to call her out of her room. When she hears the door close, she comes on her own. Her face flashes with surprise and then fear when she sees that we have a visitor. The same visitor I tricked her with before.

River smiles at her, juggling an apple between his palms.

"Hello, Isabella."

"You know my name?" she asks.

Her eyes flicker to me, and she bites her lip. She wants him to be someone other than who he really is. A knight come to save her.

She wants to tell him about her monster. How I am keeping her here against her will. About the dirty things I do to her, but not how much she really loves them. The things he has already seen with his own eyes.

"Of course I do," he answers. "My friend Javi here has told me so much about you."

My cheeks heat, and I want to tell her that's a lie. I've told River very little about her. But he is nosy. And this is his way of getting information. I have no doubt he will ask her plenty when I'm gone, while she tries to persuade him to set her free.

"I'm leaving," I announce.

Both of them look at me. River takes a bite of his apple, and Bella's eyes grow wide.

Afraid.

River is watching me carefully as I go to her, but I do not care. I touch her cheek. It has been so long since I've allowed myself to touch her. To feel her. To breathe her in.

I want her. I want her to let me have her.

"You are mine, Bella," I assure her. "Only mine."

It is the right thing to say. Her shoulders relax, and she leans into my touch. It surprises me.

River smirks. I don't care.

"Where are you going?" Bella asks.

"I have some business to take care of."

She doesn't know about Luke. She doesn't know about the trouble he has gone to in order to find her. She also doesn't know that I've been looking for her father myself. And that Luke isn't the only matter I am leaving for today.

"How long will you be gone for?"

Her lip trembles and something wrenches inside of my chest. An urge to comfort her. To tell her it's okay. But that would be a lie.

She is with me. And it is not okay.

"I will be back soon enough."

"That's what my father always used to say."

She retreats, and I feel the loss of her immediately. My hand is cold when I shove it into my pocket and turn away.

River gives me a nod before I go. One that says everything I need to know.

He will take care of her.

Chapter 24

Isabella

If Javi had a brother, it could be River. They are alike in so many ways. Both lofty and well built. Masculine. Dark. Mysterious. But where Javi is closed off, River is open.

There is something about him that alarms me. The way he smiles. It isn't normal. I don't trust that he's all there in the head. But then again, I don't trust that Javi is either, really.

And yet, I have started to feel safe with Javi. It is the story my father used to tell, becoming my own. I am the caged bird, adapting to my prison.

The guilt and confusion weigh heavy on my soul. I should want to leave. Before it's too late. It's a long shot. But I have to try.

River is eating another apple. His third since he arrived. He is at ease in Javi's home. He is at ease around me. I doubt there is anyone that can truly ruffle his feathers.

"What has Javi told you about me?" I ask.

"Very little, actually," he says between bites. "I was just giving him shit."

"So he hasn't told you?"

"Told me what?"

"That he kidnapped me? That he's holding me here against my will?"

River smiles. Unfazed. "Oh, he did tell me that."

I glare at him.

"So that's the kind of man you are? You're just going to let him do this..."

"Do what?" he asks. "You look fine to me."

"I don't want to be here," I bark. "Please, if you have any morals at all... please just let me go."

He is quiet for a moment. I think he might actually be considering it. Until he laughs.

"Do you know where I met Javi?"

"No."

"In the psych ward," he says, twirling a finger around his head. "That should tell you I'm loco, little Bella."

"You met him in the sanitarium?"

Suddenly, I'm less concerned with my escape and more interested in what he has to say.

"After he killed his mother?"

"Yep."

His reply is matter of fact. Unbothered. And I find myself wondering about him too. If he doesn't seem to mind that Javi killed his mother, I can only imagine what he was in there for.

"You know what I think?" River asks.

"What?"

"I think you like him. I think you like the mystery of him. The dangerous man beneath the hood. Have you seen him yet?"

I open my mouth to deny it. But River laughs.

"Spare me. You can lie to yourself, princess. But you were worried about him leaving you here with the big bad wolf because you feel safer with him."

"I just want to leave," I tell him.

"Do you?" he asks. "Do you really?"

"Yes."

"And go back to what? That glamorous life you hated so much? Your pervert manager who couldn't keep his mitts off you?"

"It's not any different than Javi. I've traded one hell for another."

But even as I say the words, they feel like a lie. I hate it. I hate that I am so confused about Javi. I don't understand why I feel things when he touches me. Why I dream about him sometimes. Or why I lie awake at night in my bed, listening to see if he will come down the hall to my room.

River can see this weakness inside of me. And I'm certain Javi can too.

"I'm going to go read," I mutter.

River reaches for another apple and nods. But when I enter the hallway, his words stop me.

"How do you know?"

I turn and look at him.

"What?"

"How do you know he killed his mother?"

* * *

Javi has been gone for four days. It feels like a year.

It's strange without his presence here. I'm on edge, and I don't really know why. I'm lonely and bored and the last four days have left me wordless and anxious.

River doesn't bother me.

He lounges around the house all day, eating apples and listening to music. Today I catch him looking at some of Javi's drawings. Drawings that I have only recently discovered myself. They have the same precision as the ones he used to send me.

I sit down across from River and watch him as he studies the charcoal sketches.

"What do you think they mean?"

River rolls his eyes. Laughs.

"Why does everything have to mean something? Maybe he just likes to draw."

I don't reply.

He's a smart ass. And I don't know why I even thought to bother with him at all.

I stand up. But he stops me again.

"They're tattoos."

"Tattoos?"

River pulls up his sleeve and shows off his own ink. Raises his eyebrows at me like I'm a half-wit.

"I know what tattoos are."

"Congratulations," he replies.

"You're an asshole."

"Never said I wasn't."

We fall silent. Staring at each other. I want to ask him when Javi is going to be back. It's taking too long. And I don't know why it matters, but it just does.

"He draws them," River tells me. "I ink them."

"He has tattoos?"

"You really haven't seen him," he says. "Have you?"

I shake my head. He smiles.

"Won't be long now."

I glare, and he makes a gesture with his hand.

"You can run along now. I'm bored of you."

And so continues the next three days.

River doesn't look at me. Whatever concerns I had in the beginning are long gone now. I know now that he either respects or fears Javi too much to do anything to me.

We are like ghosts in the house, living together, but not really speaking. Until the seventh day. When even he is on edge, and he comes to the conservatory and finds me reading. He walks around the room, taking in the roses and the books while eating his apple.

Quiet.

Too quiet.

"I have to go out for a little bit."

"What?"

"I have to leave for a while."

At first, I think he's joking. But it becomes obvious that this time he isn't. I'm not really concerned with the why, because this could be it. My chance.

"Okay."

He's quiet again. Thinking again. Watching me while he eats his apple.

"It's been too long."

"What do you mean?"

"He should have been back by now."

I swallow. Tell myself I don't care. It doesn't matter. Javi doesn't mean anything to me. If he's gone, then it means I can be free again. It's what I should be thinking. Instead, something else comes out of my mouth.

"Is he okay?"

River shrugs like it's not a big deal. But he looks concerned. As concerned as a psychopath can be, I suppose.

"Come with me for a minute," he says. "I need to show you something."

I close the book and stand up. He walks down the hallway, and I follow. He pauses at the door to Javi's master suite and gestures to a piece of paper on the bedside table. I move to inspect it, only to realize it was a trick when River shuts the door behind me and engages the lock.

"What the hell?"

I pound on the door.

"Let me out."

"Sorry, princess. No can do. Gotta make sure you don't cause any mischief while I'm gone."

"I won't," I lie. "Please don't leave me locked in here."

"You have everything you need in there. I'll be back soon."

"But what if you're not?" I ask. "What if something happens and you can't come back?"

Silence is the only response I get. Because he's gone. And when I turn around, I'm not any more relieved to see that he was right. He has, in fact, stocked the room with everything I could need.

For what looks like a year.

Chapter 25

Isabella

It's been three days.

Three long, never-ending days.

While River supplied me with food and books, he didn't supply me with my journal. So I have my thoughts, but nothing to write them down with.

I sing the new lyrics on repeat so that I can remember. I take baths. I eat the food he left in here for me. I attempt to read. But my mind is elsewhere. Scattered. Wondering what's happening.

Where is Javi? What is he doing?

I don't have to wonder long. On the fourth day, River returns. I want to slap him when he opens the door. But the expression on his face is grim.

"What is it?" I ask.

My stomach flips, and I'm afraid to hear whatever it is he has to say. He gestures for me to follow him. Something that didn't bode well for me before, but this time, I trust his intentions aren't trickery.

I shuffle along beside him to keep up with his long strides.

"How are you with blood?" he asks.

I stop. He turns around and sighs.

"He's been hurt."

His words urge me forward again, and we are walking in tandem now. He leads me to the conservatory. The same bed where Javi first held me captive is where he now rests, motionless. It isn't until I am close that I see him.

And I gasp.

"What happened?"

His clothes are shredded. Covered in blood and gravel.

But it's his face.

His face that is no longer hidden beneath the hood. He looks like he's sleeping. But his face is battered and swollen. He's been beaten.

Repeatedly.

"Motorcycle accident," River tells me.

I turn to him and glare.

"Don't lie to me."

"What does it matter?" River barks. "Can you help him or not?"

I hesitate. Unsure of myself.

"He should be in a hospital."

Now River really does look at me like I'm stupid.

"He can't be in a hospital, Bella. He can't ever go back to a place like that. I had to drug him just to get him back here."

Relief swells inside of me- if only briefly. He's drugged, not knocked out. That is something, I guess.

But the level of his injuries is not something I should be dealing with. He could have a concussion. He could have broken bones. There could be internal bleeding. There could be a whole host of things that I can't fix. But when I look at Javi, I know River is right.

He can't go to a hospital. He won't. Not after his mother. Not after the sanitarium.

"I'll do my best," I whisper.

River nods and gestures to the chair beside the bed. It's stacked with first aid supplies.

"I don't like to watch," he says. "Be careful of him when he wakes up. He won't be pleasant."

"You're leaving?"

"I'll just be in the kitchen."

I nod because I guess it's better this way. I don't need him here, questioning me. Watching my every move and second guessing me when I'll be doing enough of that myself.

He moves to go. And then pauses.

"Bella?"

"Yes?"

"Hurt him, and I'll kill you."

* * *

I'm never supposed to see him. He would never allow me to see him.

But right now, he is powerless. And it feels wrong, as I cut away his clothing, knowing he would not like this. But it also feels right.

I am at war with my own thoughts.

Part of me feels guilty for wanting this. For finally feeding the monster inside of me who craves this. The one who has wondered for so long what that dark figure looks like when he doesn't have a shadow to hide behind. What this killer is hiding beneath the hoods he wears.

My mind has conjured up so many different things. But my imagination never could have prepared me for the reality.

He is massive. Imposing, even in a dead sleep. And he is completely naked now except for the black jocks stretched across his hips.

His body is a mural of muscle and ink. Muscles that have been well built and well-utilized stretch over the canvas of his frame. An array of colorful ink kisses almost every visible inch of his arms and chest. He is beautiful and utterly terrifying.

I knew this all along. But confronting it in such a visually violent way is a horse of a different color.

I finally have the chance to study his face. The long, jagged scar that cuts across his forehead and all the way down to his cheek. My fingers hover over that scar. Wanting to touch. Wanting to heal.

I've always known his scars existed, but the extent of them is shocking. There are so many. Angry and red. Deep and thick. Some are small and round, others stretched and jagged. They litter his chest and abdomen, biceps and even his neck. But the most notable is the scar intersecting the crest of his dark eyebrow.

It makes him look like a warrior. And he is. Javi has been through so much. There is no denying it now. He was only a child when he was marked by these horrors.

My father never spoke of Javi's scars. There was only one time when I caught him watching the news of the events that unfolded that night. He said that it was the perfect storm of circumstances.

Those words have haunted me for so long. They have instilled within me so many questions. Doubts about the things I read in Javi's file. And perhaps justification for my baffling response to him.

My father knew Javi was dangerous, but he trusted him. He never came to harm while in his presence.

The few times my father did speak of Javi, it was with reverence. My dad was the smartest man I ever knew. And yet, he would say that Javi's mind was the most incredible thing he'd ever beheld.

At this particular moment, faced with the beast himself, I would have to disagree.

It is his body.

Though scarred and hardened, he is a work of art. One so twisted, Poe could write infinite sonnets about the darkness he carries around with him. A beautiful monster.

I can't look away from him. And I have never stared at anyone this way. He is bloodied and battered, and utterly gory. And still, he is the most captivating sight I have ever beheld.

I need to get a grip. I need to help him. Fix him. But I don't even know where to begin.

There is gravel lodged deep into the skin of his knees. His elbows. Fresh cuts litter his body. I take note of them all, categorizing them into order of severity. I decide to start with his face first. While he is still asleep.

I know that River is right. When he wakes up, he won't be happy. So, I need to work fast.

The cut on his cheek is the worst by far, and this is the one I start with. Little by little, I cleanse the blood from his face with a wet cloth. Seeing him in a different light.

He is still rigid. So rough around the edges. His beard is wild, and so is his long dark hair, pulled back into an untidy bun. It's an odd thing. I had no idea his hair was so long.

I wonder when it was last cut. And then I realize, he has nobody to cut it for him. But when I smooth it away from his face, I also realize it doesn't need to be cut. Not really.

He's a Neanderthal. But it works for him. For his masculine bone structure. His oversized frame. Even with all of his hardness, there is still something soft about him too. At least like this. When he's asleep. His face is relaxed. At peace.

His lips soft and full, and his nose strong. His skin is softer than I expected. Naturally olive in complexion. His hair and his beard are dark. But even those are soft.

I drink in his features while I can. Pausing my work every so often just to stare at him. To try to make sense of this beast of a man before me. But he is a puzzle I still haven't figured out.

And there isn't time now.

I feel him beginning to stir. When I go to work on the gravel, drawing it from his skin, he wakes completely. There isn't time to prepare myself for his reaction. It is instinctive.

A wounded predator, cornered.

He launches his hand upright and seizes me by the throat. His breathing is harsh. Labored. And his eyes are vulnerable. So vulnerable. The wildest eyes I have ever seen.

"Javi."

My hand covers his, but I don't struggle with him. I don't resist. He needs reassurance right now. And that's what I intend to give him.

"Javi, it's okay. I'm trying to help. You are injured. I'm just trying to help."

His brow furrows when he glances down at his body. His almost naked body. Shame washes over his features, and his grip on me loosens if only a little.

"Leave me," he roars.

He is trying to intimidate me. But he can't. Not this time.

"No."

His eyes meet mine. Fiery. Confused.

Frightened.

"I'm going to tend to your wounds, Javi. Whether you like it or not. So please don't fight me."

His hand trembles around my neck, and then slowly his fingers fall away. He is quiet. Still. And now I am the one shaking as I go back to work, pulling the gravel from his wounds.

He hisses when I hit a tender spot, and I apologize. I am gentle with him. As gentle as I can be. But I know it still hurts. He doesn't like me seeing him this way. He is ashamed. Embarrassed. But he has no reason to be.

He did not cause these scars on his body.

I want to tell him that he shouldn't care what anyone thinks. But it is easier to say than to know how he must feel, living with such scars.

"Why are you doing this?" he asks. "Why are you helping me?"

The words are on the tip of my tongue. The words I should say, to protect myself. I should remain stubborn and indignant. Rebellious to my situation.

I could tell him that River threatened to kill me. That I had no choice. But those aren't the words that leave my lips.

"I can't just leave you here like this, Javi. Someone needs to take care of you too."

"I don't need anyone to take care of me," he growls.

And now he is the one who is stubborn and indignant.

I smile up at him. But it is not mocking. It is just that I never thought I could relate to him. But at this moment, I can.

"Everybody needs some help sometimes, Javi. Even men like you."

"You mean monsters like me."

I shake my head.

"I don't think you are nearly as monstrous as you make yourself out to be."

His eyes move over me, but he does not reply. He does not say another word. Until I am finished. When he asks me for something else. He asks me for some clothes.

It is a softly spoken request. A difficult one for him to make. I don't fight him on it. But when I return from his room, he is not happy with the selection I brought him.

A pair of black sweats and a tee shirt.

"A hoodie," he demands, his polite demeanor gone.

"No."

I cross my arms and hold my ground.

"I have seen you now. River has seen you. There is no reason for you to hide."

He glares at me.

"You would choose to look at me this way?" he sneers.

"Yes," I answer without hesitation. "I would prefer to see your face when I speak to you, Javi."

He does not believe me. He thinks it is a trick. And my heart hurts that he feels this way. I don't want to feel bad for him. I don't want to sympathize with him. But I do.

I know better than anyone what it's like to be so critical of yourself. To believe the nasty things people say about you. I know what it's like to feel ugly inside and out.

I know what it's like to be a monster too.

Javi might not know it, but there is still humanity left inside of him. There is still good. And I don't know if he deserves it, but I want to fight his demons with him. I want to prove to him once and for all that these scars don't matter to me. That the things I say and do are not a trick as he would like to believe.

I'm not even certain what his reaction will be. Or how far I am willing to go. But I only know that it feels right when I kneel beside him on the bed and straddle his hips.

He is hard beneath me, already. His breath still and silent when he looks up at me.

I slide the strap of my tank top over my shoulder until it falls, repeating on the other side. The material pools around my waist, revealing my bra.

Javi watches me, growing in size and hardness beneath me.

I unbuckle the clasp, and it falls away. I am naked from the waist up. My breasts are heavy and tender and cold. I reach for his hands, and he lets me guide them to me. He touches me, groaning when I rock against him with my hips. There is still a barrier between us. His jocks and my panties. It feels safer this way.

And also more forbidden.

We are so close, but not quite skin to skin. It doesn't matter to Javi. He fondles me roughly in his calloused hands. Groping my breasts and then wrenching me forward to kiss him.

His mouth is hungry, and so is mine. I drink him in. I taste him. And I move against him. It becomes frenzied. Both of us forgetting the extent of his injuries until one of his wounds reopens, and he starts to bleed again.

I move to stop. To apologize. Javi clutches my hip and forces me to keep going.

"I like it," he tells me.

The pain. He likes the pain. It concerns me. It excites me. It makes me want to hurt him and please him all at once. But Javi is in control now. Even from the bottom. He grasps my hips and forces my movements. Using me as the warmth and friction he so badly needs.

I am a prisoner in his arms again. But I am free. Free to my sordid desires. I lean back and press my hand against his cut, applying pressure.

Too much pressure.

I give him the pain he needs. And then I pull away. His eyes darken when he sees the way his blood stains my skin.

He is feral again. Seizing my bloody palm to smear it down between my breasts, marking me with his blood. I whimper, and he comes. For what feels like forever. His body purging itself of the pain inside of him.

He kisses me again. And then releases me.

For a moment, I don't move. I don't want to. I want to stay here with him, like this. I don't understand it. I don't know what's wrong with me or why I want him this way. But I can't control it, and I can no longer deny it.

Javi is tired. His eyes are heavy and relaxed. But the longer we sit here, staring at one another, the more the tension creeps back into his body all over again. So I move from him. Slowly.

I clean his wound again and then reach for his jocks. He grabs my wrist.

"I'll do it."

He doesn't want me to touch him again. Because he's exhausted and afraid he won't be able to control himself if I do. It's there in his eyes. And I had no idea how open his eyes could be until now.

"You should get some rest," I tell him. "I will make something for dinner."

I turn to go, and he stops me again with his hand.

"Bella?"

He looks up at me, anxious.

"Thank you."

Chapter 26

Isabella

I make Spaghetti for dinner. River digs in as soon as he smells it. Javi is a different story.

When I take the tray to the conservatory, he is still sleeping. I hover, unsure whether to wake him or not. He senses me before I can make a decision and his eyes open slowly.

He is defensive again. Wearing the sweats I brought him earlier along with a hoodie that I didn't bring him. It is obvious he has made his own way to the closet, and I make a mental note to take care of that problem as soon as I leave him tonight.

"Are you hungry?" I ask.

He tries to sit up, wincing as he props himself against the headboard.

"What is it?"

"Spaghetti."

"I don't eat spaghetti," he says.

"Have you ever tried it?"

He doesn't reply.

I sit down beside him, and he reaches for the tray. I pull it back.

"Let me help you."

"I don't need your help."

"Then you don't eat."

He growls, and I ignore him. I couldn't imagine him attempting to eat this himself after the way I saw him eat before.

I twirl some pasta on the fork and bring it to his lips. He's still staring at me. Being stubborn.

"Open."

He opens, reluctantly. I feed him and tell him to chew slowly. He listens this time, watching me carefully. When he swallows, I ask him how he likes it.

"It's... fine."

I'm relieved. It's silly. But I want him to like it. I want him to experience something else besides peanut butter and jelly or macaroni and cheese. He eats the entire plate I brought him and then relaxes back against the bed.

"Will you tell me what happened to you?"

He stares at me. Guarded.

"It was nothing."

"It's not nothing," I argue. "Is this because of the agency?"

I can't hide the worry in my voice. The worry that he will end up like my father too.

"I can't tell you that."

It's the same generic response my father used to give and I know I'm right. I hate that I'm right. And I miss my father so much my heart feels like it's splintered.

I hate the agency. I hate them for taking him away from me. For lying to me. And I am angry at Javi too, right now. For not having the consideration to think that he might do the same one day.

That he might just disappear, and then...

Then I would be free.

It hurts to think about. I look at him, uncertain. He is confused too, by my response. By my emotions.

"I am sorry, Bella," he says.

And he is sorry, but for what I don't know.

"How can you work for them?" I ask. "Knowing that they don't care. That you might meet the same fate. How can you do it?"

He raises his brows, reaches for me, but stops himself.

"I am not going anywhere."

"That's funny," I tell him. "Because it's the same thing my father always used to say."

"Your father did not want to leave you," he says. "He did not do it by choice."

"I understand that," I snap. "But the very agency that he has risked his life for refuses to tell me anything. For all I know, they want him to stay gone."

"Bella," Javi says, and this time he does touch me. "Your father was not the man that you imagine in your head. He has many secrets. And many enemies too."

His words are not meant to hurt me this time. I can tell by the way he says them. But he believes them wholeheartedly. And I still can't accept this when I know how much my father cared for him. I can't comprehend what happened between them to make Javi hate him so much.

But I'm tired of guessing. Avoiding. And I know he won't be this agreeable forever. So if Javi wants to tell me some truths about my father, perhaps it's time for me to listen.

My fingers fall into my lap, and I lean back in my chair.

"Will you tell me about him?" I whisper. "Will you tell me about your relationship?"

Chapter 27

Javier

Her eyes are soft. Hopeful. I can't deny her.

It would be better that she did not know. It would be better if she did not ask these things of me. But she has seen me. Touched me. And I want her to do it again.

I want to give her the answers she seeks. The only thing I can ever really give her after the things I have done.

"What would you care to know, my sweet?"

"How did you meet?" she asks.

It is an innocent question. And because my Bella is so innocent, she could never know the depths of her father's depravity. She could never know the injustices he served to not only me but countless others. And she could never know the deepness of the despair this memory invokes in me.

I will forever remember the day that I met Ray Rossi.

He found his way into my room at the sanitarium, and I assumed he was another doctor. Someone else sent to pry the secrets from my mind. But he was different. Both in dress and decorum.

He was powerful.

He told the nurse to go, and she listened, hesitating only briefly at the door. She informed him that I was dangerous. He met my eyes and smiled.

"He is a child."

The nurse left, and Ray sat down with me. He wasn't like the others. He did not ask me questions. He did not ask me to talk.

Instead, he handed me a workbook. It had puzzles and math equations. Things that I liked. I wondered how he knew.

I had done some of my own, on the paper they sometimes let me have. The doctor would stare at my scribbles strangely. He tried to make sense of them, I think, but he never could.

This man, though, he understood. And this is exactly what I tell my Bella.

"He brought me puzzles."

"At the sanitarium?" she asks.

I nod.

She waits quietly. Hoping for more. I don't know what to tell her. There are so many things. Things I have waited to say.

Hateful things. Painful things. Things that tear at the very fabric of the man I am now.

I want her to know what a coward her father is. I want her to hate him as much as I do. To understand that given a choice, he would probably betray her too.

He would rather leave her here with me than risk his own life to get her back because that's the kind of man he is. But for as long as I've waited to say these things, I can't seem to tell her now. Not yet.

"He brought them to me every week."

"So you liked the puzzles," she says. "I see you working on them sometimes, around the house."

"Yes."

"Because you're smart, Javi."

I don't reply.

My mother always said I was smart because I was good at science. Like her. But I was never good at people.

"And then what happened?" Bella asks.

I try to recall the exact order of events. The time that I was locked away, and for how long. At first, I had counted the days and weeks and months. But when Ray started coming to visit and bringing me the workbooks, the counting ceased. I spent my free time completing the books. They became more and more challenging over the course of his visits. And I always wanted more.

Sometimes, I completed them too soon, and I had to wait days for another. Until finally there was a day that Ray came back, and he wasn't alone. He had a different man with him this time. And he asked me for the workbook. The workbook that had been the most complicated one he'd ever brought me so far.

I gave it to him. He smiled like he was proud of me. He hadn't even checked it yet. But he told the other man he didn't need to.

He handed it off to the stranger who inspected it with a furrowed brow. That man looked at me, uncertain.

"This can't be right," he'd said. "He's only a boy."

Ray laughed and handed me another workbook.

"Javi, can you do me a favor?"

He opened up the book and pointed to a page.

"Can you solve this one for me?"

I took the pen he provided and solved it in ten minutes while they watched. The man beside him was smiling too when I finished.

"Well, I'll be damned."

They looked at each other, and then to me.

"So?" Ray asked. "How about it?"

"I think perhaps you are right," the man said. "I think he will make an excellent addition to the program."

Ray looked at me and nodded.

"Indeed."

I didn't know it then, but my life was about to change. It was about to get better, for the first time in a long time. I didn't know then that I would grow to hate Bella's father so much. I didn't know the kind of man that he was. Because he showed me something else at first. Something I needed at the time, in a world where nobody understood me.

The man who gave me guidance and a purpose. The man who took me away from the sanitarium. He never treated me like I was dangerous. He helped me with my anger. He helped me as much as he could. He did everything he could to help me.

And now here I am, holding his most beloved daughter captive in my home.

When I think of those early days, and how much I cared for Ray- how much I respected him- it hurts to think of what has become of us.

I can't uncross the lines I have already breached. I can't undo the moments I caved beneath the weight of my darkness and gave into temptation. But what I can do is be honest with her. I can try to make her understand. At least some of it.

Until I'm ready to give her the truth.

"It was never about leaving you," I tell her. "Or choosing me."

She looks at me, eyes shining, and then hides them beneath a veil of hair.

"That isn't what it felt like. He left me to go to you. He did it all the time."

"Because he was responsible for me," I explain. "And he was teaching me. It was only part of his job."

She glances up at me, and her eyes are still wet, but it isn't for herself.

"You were never just a job to him, Javi. Surely, you must know that. He cared about you as if you were his own son."

His own son.

Those words hit me hard. Much harder than I could anticipate. I knew that he was proud of me. I knew that he felt responsible for me. But I also know why he took on the burden of helping me.

I did not live with him as a son would. I was kept separate. Alone.

He came to visit me at the program, and I kept to my routine. I did what he asked of me, and I excelled at everything he put in front of me. Because I wanted to make him proud.

At the time, I felt indebted to him. For saving me from that place. And for saving River too when I had requested it.

He had given me so much.

I never had a father. But hearing Bella say those words makes me feel as though perhaps I did. Perhaps I did see him that way, and I just never knew it until now.

And now, there is a foreign sensation inside of me when I look at my Bella. So soft and sweet and broken. Caring for me after all that I have done to her.

She is inherently good.She sees past my ugliness. My feelings for her are split.

I want to hurt her. But I want to protect her too. And I think that perhaps she was right. I think the person she most needs protection from is me.

"What are you thinking about, Javi?" she asks.

I don't like that she can see me so well. That even beneath the hood I have replaced, she can read me. It's strange, not being able to hide anymore.

It makes me feel exposed. I want to forget that she has seen all of me. That she has witnessed my scars. I wonder if they haunt her. If she cringes when she thinks of them. But I cannot tell her these things.

"I'm thinking about what your father would say," I reply. "If he knew you were here."

She is quiet. Lost in her own thoughts as she studies me.

"Sometimes, I don't know what my father would say," she admits. "I love him very much. But I feel like I don't know him very well. He had so many secrets. And I have wondered..."

She threads her fingers together in her lap and looks into my eyes again.

"Wondered what?" I press.

"I have wondered what he did to you, Javi."

I do not answer her.

Bella rises from her chair and moves towards me.

My pulse quickens.

She approaches me the way one would approach a wild animal. My fists are locked at my side, my muscles tense. Her arm trembles and her lip does too. She raises my hood and pushes it back away from my face.

My body is still sore. Still healing. And it looks worse than usual.

I don't like this. I don't like her seeing me like this. I move to grab her wrist. But she is fast this time. And determined.

"No, Javi," she says. "I want to see you. Let me see you."

My body goes on the offensive. Every muscle tightening and contracting. Every instinct inside of me demanding that I eliminate the threat. But one look into Bella's eyes gives me the control I need to restrain myself.

My hand falls back to my side. And I let her see me. I cannot deny this angel.

She moves between my legs. Hesitates. Now it feels as though she is the predator. She sits on my lap, and her palm comes up to touch my face.

I close my eyes when she maps out the scars with her fingertip. I don't like it. But I don't want her to stop either.

"Bella."

My voice is hoarse. Strained. I don't know what I need from her. But my Bella knows. She leans in and kisses me. She kisses my scars, healing me in some way. As though they could disappear beneath her gentle touch.

I know that they can't. But it feels like they are. Like she is the cure to my disease. Her lips find mine. I can't be gentle with her anymore. I catch her face in my hands and kiss her violently. She whimpers but does not protest.

I am hard for her. So fucking hard. I grind my hips into her soft flesh and want so badly to feel her from the inside. I want to destroy her and fill her with my come.

I want her to cry so I can taste her tears. I want her to make me bleed. I don't know how to make it stop. I can't cure this madness in my head.

I'm not supposed to want her this way. I'm not supposed to feel anything when I look at her.

Her hands are on me. On my skin. Beneath my shirt. Touching me. Feeling me. Burning and healing me.

"Take off your sweater," she begs. "Please, Javi."

I look into her eyes, seeking out the deception I am certain to find there. But it is absent.

"Please," she says again.

I push my hand between her legs. Cupping her through the leggings. She is wet for me. For the monster beneath her. I don't understand it. How can she want something so bad for her?

"Javi."

She's pulling up the sweater herself now.

My mind is still at war, but my body is responding to her. Lifting my arms up when she tells me. My sweater ends up on the floor, and my chest is bare for her. Hard and scarred to her soft and pure.

Her palms move over me, exploring. Her lips find the skin of my throat first. And then my collar bone. Then the scars that litter my body. I close my eyes, and my head falls back against the chair.

She is the only one I've ever allowed to touch me in this way. I would not have believed that it was possible. That it could be real.

But it is.

I am allowing her to touch me, and she is wet for me.

"You have always been mine," I tell her.

Her hand moves down to the bulge in my sweatpants, cupping the hard heat through the material.

"But what about you, Javi?" she asks. "Does that mean you are mine, too?"

I groan when she squeezes me through the material, my self-control hanging on by a thread. She leans forward in my lap and kisses my neck again. All the way up to my ear.

"Let me have you," she says. "Let me have all of you."

Chapter 28

Isabella

Javi's fingers dig into my hips, his eyes sharp and intense.
"You don't know what you're asking for."
"I do," I tell him, and it's a lie.
I know Javi is fucked up in the head. I know that he is a well of darkness I haven't even tapped into yet. And I fear those parts of him. But I am also drawn to it.

The darkness in him speaks to the darkness in me.

The space between us is loud with energy, boiling over into our heated skin.

"Get up," he tells me.

I hesitate.

Afraid he is going to reject me. Afraid he is going to send me away. It isn't what I want. I don't know how to convince him otherwise.

He reaches up and snags a handful of my hair in his grip.

"Are you going to do what you're told, Bella?"

His voice is menacing and hot. Hungry and full of promise. He's on the verge of breaking. And I think he just might give in.

So I stand, and he releases his grip on my hair, lifting his hips up to remove his sweat pants. I try to help him, and he growls at me.

"Do as you are told, Bella. Be a good girl."

I let him do it, even though it's obvious he is in pain. He removes his pants and slides to the edge of the bed, swinging his legs over so that his feet rest on the floor and his hands are at his sides.

"Now come here."

I come to him, still fully clothed. Javi directs me with short, precise commands. He tells me to remove my shirt. And I do. Then my pants.

I do.

I'm standing before him in my bra and panties, and he's on the verge of losing control. I want him to. So I provoke him by removing the rest without his permission.

I am naked before him. Naked and cold and vulnerable.Something I have never liked to be. I don't know why I like it so much right now.

Javi's palm spreads over my hip and slides up my rib cage to cup my breast, his thumb skating across my nipple. I jerk forward like I'm being pulled by a magnet. Crushing against his body heat, and still not close enough.

He is a composition of hard muscle and painted tattoos. His cock, rigid and swollen against his thigh.

He's a monster. A chillingly hot monster. And I want him. I want him so badly it hurts deep in my core. He's going to ruin me. Destroy me. Physically and mentally. I know this. And yet I beg him for it, even as he shoves me to my knees before him.

"Kiss me."

I kiss him.

On the head of his cock.

The moisture of his arousal slides over my lips, and I part them to lick it off. In doing so, my tongue brushes against the head of his cock, and he groans.

As with all things, Javi does not have the patience for me to take him softly or slowly. He grabs my head and shoves himself deep into my throat, gagging me.

He holds me there, testing me. My hands rest on his thighs, and I don't dare move. I don't even breathe. I remain silent and still, my eyes watering while he measures my limits.

"Is this what you want, little Bella?"

I try to nod, but I can't move my head under the force of his grip. He sighs and releases me, allowing me to fill my lungs.

I look up at him. He expects animosity. Hopes for it. Anything to stop this. His eyes are pleading with me. Begging me to have some sense. To understand that he is a monster. To understand that I am asking him to destroy me. My eyes implore him to do it. To do the thing my lips can't speak of.

I rest my cheek against his thigh, stroking my fingers over the scarred skin there. The still raw wounds of his new injuries. Pressing a little harder than I should. Giving him the thing I know he wants and craves. The pain.

He shudders. Petting my hair beneath his palm while I trace the sensitive flesh with my nails. And I know. I know he's going to give into me now. He can't help himself. He reaches for something on the bedside table, and I don't see it until it flashes beneath the light.

The edge of the metal blade presses against my throat, dragging over the skin there. My heart accelerates, and my eyes snap up to his.

One push and he could end my life right now. I already know him to be a murderer. He murdered his own mother. But it's his eyes that give him away. This is his last attempt at pushing me away. He wants me to be afraid. He wants at least one of us to come to our senses.

I reach up and rest my hand over the blade. Gently, he allows me to remove it from his grip.

I press it against his thigh. Javi's eyes heat and his cock jumps. He wants this. He wants this fucked up scenario more than anything. He wants me to do the very thing his mother did to him.

I should stop. I should run away. I should reason that they were right to put him away. To lock him up and institutionalize him. But the need inside of him calls out to me.

And instead of appealing to logic, I dig the blade into his flesh. I dig until it pierces the skin and crimson oozes from the wound.

His lungs are at a standstill when I move my free palm between his legs to stroke his cock. He grunts. Bucks into my hand. Tosses the knife away and yanks me up onto the bed.

He is still bleeding from his thigh, and I wonder if I did too much. If I went too far. If I crossed a line I won't be able to uncross.

These thoughts all crash through my mind in jarring succession while he positions himself over me and secures my wrists above my head. I don't even know what he bound them with until I see the ropes around the bed frame.

The fear is potent when I pull against them and can't move.

"Javi," I plead with him, my voice betraying my terror. "Please..."

"I warned you, Bella," he says. "I told you."

He reaches for the knife. I squeeze my eyes shut and tremble beneath him. The tip rests against my collar bone, trailing along the sensitive flesh before it dips lower. Onto my chest, directly above my breast.

"My turn."

He cuts into my flesh, and I don't make a sound. Javi is breathing hard enough for both of us, his voice heavy with arousal when he speaks.

"Open your eyes."

I open my eyes.

The ache is intense. Euphoric. I feel lightheaded. High. And I can't tell if I am afraid or turned on when I glance down at the red line on my chest.

It is only small. Superficial. Enough to draw blood. I thought it would be worse. It felt so much worse.

Javi leans forward, pressing his skin into mine. He kisses me. It's so fucking wrong to like this. That's what I keep telling myself. It's so fucking wrong what he's doing to me. I know it. He knows it. But we can't help ourselves.

I am at his mercy as he drags his lips down my throat and sucks my nipple into his mouth. He licks me until I am raw and drenched with need. And then he pulls my legs up around his hips, opening me up wide for him.

It hurts already, and he hasn't even entered me. I look up at him and plead with my eyes. I want to ask him to be gentle. I want to tell him to just take me.

It doesn't matter though because Javi does what he wants. He drags his cock through my arousal and pushes inside of me.

"Javi."

He thrusts deep.

I freeze. Burn. Cry.

He collects my tears with his lips.

"My Bella." He rocks his hips into me. "My Bella."

I squirm beneath him, uncertain whether I'm trying to break free or get closer. His eyes find mine, soft and warm and golden. They are so different now. He is changing before my eyes. The icy walls around his heart are thawing, and it's because of me.

His fingers brush over my cheek. My lips. Full of worship. I squeeze closer to him, and his eyes flutter shut. The pain of our past fades beneath the soothing touch of his fingers on my skin. His lips on my neck. His body in mine.

I ache to touch him. I beg him to free me from my restraints, but my pleas go ignored as he reaches down to touch me.

He makes me come with several strokes of his fingers. It isn't violent this time. It is a slow, lingering burn that stays with me while he sucks on my throat, marking me. Claiming me.

He is bare inside of me, the way he always has been. Raw. I should tell him to pull out. I should be worried. Scared. Logical. But I can't be any of those things with Javi.

I am drunk on the kool-aid. Intoxicated by him.

My lips part against his throat. Breathing him in. I'm going to tell him to be smart. To think about this. That's what I'm going to do. But the words come out of my mouth wrong. So, so wrong. And so, so right.

"Come inside of me, Javi."

He bucks against me and thrusts all the way inside, jerking as he empties himself deep in my womb. Filling me with his come. Filling me with poisonous thoughts.

I want him. I hate him.

My feelings for him are a battlefield.

And the only refuge I have is that when he looks down at me, I can see the same reflected back in his eyes.

Chapter 29

Javier

My Bella always tastes so sweet when she is like this. When she is pliable and sated and filled with my come. Her tits red and swollen from my beard and my tongue. Her chest dried with blood. And a cut that I trace with my finger, wondering if it will leave a scar.

She is still bound at the wrists, but she no longer begs me to let her go. When she looks at me now, there is warmth in her eyes. Warmth that lies and lures me in. Warmth designed to make me let my guard down.

She is still trying to deceive me. I am certain. How could she ever love the beast that I am? My body and mind are tired of this war raging on inside of my head.

I untie her and lay beside her. She touches my chest with her fingertips. Hesitant. Anxious.

There is a part of me that feels shame for that. For making her fearful. For making her question me. That same part of me wants to tell her that it's okay. That she need not ever be afraid of me again.

But that would be a lie.

And unlike her father, I am a man of my word. I may not have honor, but the one thing I will not do to my Bella is lie to her now. I will not give her false hope where none can live.

For tonight only, I will hold her. Comfort her. And in the morning, she can learn all over again why it is unwise to trick me.

* * *

Sunlight warms the back of my eyelids, and for a moment, I have forgotten where I am.

My body is stiff and sore. A reminder of the events that have unfolded over the last several days. A reminder of another sacrifice I have made for this girl. One that I cannot fully comprehend.

My intentions were simple. I would go to Luke and buy out her contract. I would tell him that she was done. He was never to speak her name in the media again.

It should have been simple. But what I did not anticipate was that Luke was expecting me. That I would be greeted at his door by seven armed guards. And that I would be held there while they tried to beat their answers out of me.

It was an irony I could not help but find amusing. I told Luke as much when he tried to punch me in the face. He doesn't know the meaning of torture. And there was not a thing he could do that would ever make me tell him where my Bella was.

I had already been subjected to torture on a level that Luke's mind could never grasp.

In the end, his guards were weak and ignorant. Luke was a slave to his addictions. Coming and going at all hours of the night, fueling his body with the drugs he needed to function.

His guards got lazy. The beatings became careless. Lacking heart and spirit. Eventually, they became indifferent too, as they led me to the bathroom. They thought me weak. And that was the last thought they had before I killed them.

All but Luke.

Him, I am saving for another time. When I have regained my strength. When I can question him and find out who is at the root of this betrayal.

I think of my Bella. I think of how she tricks me with her soft touches and warm looks. She could not have known my intentions for leaving. But I want to believe it is her. That she is the traitor at the root of this.

It is easier to believe than any of the other scenarios in my mind. That I have been so careless not to have noticed I was followed.

That the agency is watching me, and they are perhaps

connected to Luke. These are all questions I have. And the answers have not yet come to me. But today... today they will.

I will remember why I am doing this. I will remember that Bella is nothing to me. The only way this game can end is for me to destroy her before I deliver her fractured soul back to Ray. The same way that he destroyed me.

I take a deep breath and open my eyes, recoiling at the brightness of the conservatory. Her scent still surrounds me. But when I roll over, she is not there.

My blood roars as betrayal rages through me. She is trying to escape. Trying to trick me. All of her words the night before... lies. Her touches... lies. Her soft glances and her acceptance of what I am...

Lies.

And she will pay for it like she has never paid for anything else before.

Chapter 30

Isabella

I'm in the bathroom, digging through the drawers when a shadow passes over the frame, and I look up. Javi is there, stark naked. A powerhouse of muscle and ink. Muscles rippling with tension and golden eyes that are molten with anger.

Those wild eyes move over me, cataloging every detail and trying to piece something together in his own mind. I'm in nothing more than a towel myself, fresh from the shower, wet hair hanging down my back.

He glances at the brush in my right hand, and the dress I've picked out for today draped over the chair. He watches me carefully. Full of suspicion.

He wants to lash out at me. He wants to believe that I am tricking him again. That I was planning to leave. To run away while I had the chance. There is no point in trying to reassure him. He would not believe me, no matter what I said to him right now. So I go about the business of brushing my hair while he watches from the doorway.

"What is it you think you are doing?" he snaps.

"Getting dressed," I answer.

I can see his longing to punish me. To hurt me. To push me away. But I also see the relief hidden behind those harsh emotions. I've seen him vulnerable now, and it has changed everything between us.

Even now, the tension still lingers. The chemistry that neither one of us can deny. His palm throbs with the craving to pull me closer. To keep me at arm's length so I can never run away from him. But I think that even Javi knows he is powerless to this force now.

He is softening. Bit by bit, I am chipping away at his armor. At his insecurities. I have seen this transformation. I have no intentions of stopping it.

I point to the comb and scissors laid out on the counter.

"I thought I might give you a haircut today," I tell him softly. "If you'd like."

His eyes move over the comb and then my face. I won't get a firm yes from him. I can already feel him slipping away. It needs to be now. I walk to him and take him by the hand. A hand that is so much larger than mine. A hand that can inflict pain and pleasure in equal amounts.

I stroke my thumb over his palm and smile up at him. Soft. Vulnerable. Nervous. I want him to say yes.

I pull on his arm, and he follows. And when I gesture to the chair next to the sink, he sits.

The chair is small, and he is large. Still naked. He doesn't like it. So I remove my towel and wrap it around his shoulders before placing another over his lap. Towels so large they swallow me whole look like mere scraps on him.

I spread his long hair out and reach for the comb. I don't know how much he'll let me cut off. I don't know if he's even had a haircut since he was a child.

"How short would you like it?" I ask.

He's quiet. Tense. Annoyed.

"Just cut it all off," he answers.

So I cut. And I cut some more. And I keep cutting, waiting for him to erupt. But he never does. When it's short enough, I pull the electric razor from the drawer and start to trim.

It's a long process. But he does not complain. The longer I work, the more relaxed he becomes. When I am finished with his hair, I move onto his beard. Trimming it to a more manageable level. One that highlights the strong features of his face, but still hides the scars lurking beneath.

And when I am finished, I hand him a mirror. He stares at his reflection for a long time. I don't know what to expect. I don't know if he likes it.

He simply hands me back the mirror and grunts.

"Are you done?"

"Yes."

He gets up and tells me to finish getting dressed while he walks down the hall to his own room.

I know what will come next. I hasten to put on my dress and wait for it. I wait for his fury. His yelling. And just as I feared, he appears in the doorway a moment later. This time, he is clothed in jeans and a tee shirt. But his fists are locked at his sides. The vein in his neck is pulsing. And his eyes are lasered in on me.

"Where are they?" he demands.

"You don't need them anymore," I whisper.

He stalks towards me, and I scurry back until I hit the wall behind me. He corners me and grabs my face, rough and dominant.

"Where. Are. They?" he roars.

It takes every ounce of courage I can muster to do what I do next.

I yell back at him. The way he always yells at me.

"You. Don't. Need. Them."

He stares at me in disbelief. Then annoyance. And I wait for it. Wait for him to blow. To flip. To say he's going to punish me. To threaten me and scold me and have his way with me like he always does. But this time, he is waning.

There is uncertainty in his eyes. He wants to believe me. And I am not about to let this opportunity pass me by.

"I have already seen you," I tell him again. "There is no reason for you to be lurking around here with your face covered in shadow all the time. Especially not now that you've had a haircut."

He searches my eyes. Looks for the lies hidden within my words. I take him by the hands again, and he lets me. He lets me touch his face.

"Is it so wrong of me to want to see you?" I ask. "Can you not believe that perhaps I am telling the truth, Javi? That perhaps I actually find you incredibly handsome."

He doesn't respond, so I continue.

"Things are always worse in our own minds," I remind him. "You should know this better than anyone. The way you exposed my fears and exploited them when you brought me here. The words you played on repeat. The ones you knew would hurt me most."

He looks away. And for the briefest moment, I thought I saw shame in his eyes. But he does not voice it. He does not allow me to witness it again, either.

"Your scars mean nothing to me, Javi. Please. I am only asking you to try it."

"I want them back," he says again.

But his voice has lost the harshness from before, and he does not demand that I bring him the hoodies now.

Instead, he simply leaves the room.

Chapter 31

Isabella

Javi locks himself in the office over the course of the next three days.

He has not asked me for his hoodies again. From the rare glimpses I get when I catch him in the hall, I know he is walking around without them.

I am lonely.

There is a hunger inside of me that I can't defy. I ache for his body against mine. The smell of his skin. The vibrations of his voice. I lay in bed at night and wonder what he's doing. I wonder how to break through the walls he has built so high around his heart.

And then I wonder why I want to. Why am I still so broken for him? So willing to overlook the things he has done.

My mind and heart are divided.

I don't know how to find peace with either decision when they both hurt so much. It is ripping me apart. I can love him or hate him, but I can't go on feeling both.

I write in my journal. I play at my piano. And I sing songs with words only he can hear. But still, he does not come.

My heart is melancholy, and I think of my father too often. I wonder where he is. If he's even still alive. I wonder what he would tell me to do if he were here now. Then I remember it wouldn't matter. Because I have always been on my own. Even when he was there, the solitude was an ever-present guest. He was consumed with work, and I was consumed with vying for his attention.

My soul is tormented by the mystery of his fate. The

unknowns that still linger. But even so, there is peace in my bones. Peace that wasn't there before.

I am at ease with the knowledge that Javi needed him too, in his younger years. Regardless of whatever happened between them, Javi did love my father once. He looked up to him. And I know my father loved him too.

Now, only questions remain. Questions I am not certain I will ever have the answers to. Not until Javi is ready to share them.

The doorbell rings again this afternoon, and this time I do not race to see who it is. Javi locks eyes with me before he moves towards the door. Searching for what he is so certain he will find there.

Hope.

Hope that someone else has come to save me. But that is not what he sees. I know, because it is not what I feel. I ignore the visitor and continue the business of writing new lyrics.

It is only River anyway. He comes into the kitchen to snatch an apple from the counter before he follows Javi into his office. They shut the door behind them and remain there for an hour. And when River leaves again, Javi emerges.

Agitated.

He looks at me, and I do not like what I see there. I don't like the doubt in his eyes. The shift in his mood. He seems cold now. Shut down. I think he's going to punish me again. He's going to push me away or hurt me. But that isn't what he does.

He goes to the gym. And stays there for two hours.

Punishing himself instead.

* * *

I'm somewhere between worlds when Javi startles me by removing the book from my hands and setting it on the table beside me.

The conservatory is dark now, apart from the glittering lights of the stars above and a solitary lamp on the table beside me. The roses are fragrant, and the air is warm, and there is something else in the room between us.

A new energy. A strange energy. An exciting energy.

Javi bends down and scoops me into his arms, carrying me to

the bathroom. He places me on my feet again and removes my clothes before starting the bath.

I don't question his actions.

We are both silent when he helps me into the bath and begins to wash me. Shampooing my hair and cleaning my body with his hands. When he is finished, he moves to pull the plug, but I stop him.

"Don't," I plead.

His eyes are absent of the turmoil I saw there earlier. He is softer now. And I don't want to waste these moments, which are so rare with him.

"Will you let me wash you?"

He is silent and still for a long while. Too silent. Too still. I don't know what he's going to do. Not until he removes his shirt and unbuttons his jeans and discards them on the floor beside my own clothes.

Then he climbs in behind me, pulling me into his arms. He does not let me wash him. But he holds me. And that is more than I had hoped for.

Chapter 32

Isabella

When the water is cold, Javi helps me from the tub. He dries my hair with a towel and then my body too. He uses the same towel on himself, and I watch.

Then he takes me by the hand and leads me back into the library in the conservatory. He pulls one of the chairs onto the hardwood floor and cups my face in his palm.

"Do you know what I need from you, my Bella?"

His voice is gentle. Filled with want. And it doesn't matter what he needs from me because whatever it is, I will do it.

I nod. He kisses me.

"Good girl," he says. "Now stay right here."

I stay in place while he walks back across the room and returns a moment later with a cup in hand. A cup that I recognize well from my early days with him.

It is filled with dry rice. Rice that he scatters on the floor beneath me. I swallow and look up into his eyes when he is finished. Wondering if he is angry. Wondering if I've done something wrong.

But that isn't what I find. Today, I only see need. He needs this from me. And so when he asks me to kneel, I do it without question. It has been a long time since he punished me this way, and I have forgotten the pain. But I bear it.

For Javi.

For Javi, I would bear anything. The thought scares me. Excites me. Confuses me.

He sits in the chair in front of me. Naked. Hard. Swollen. He spreads his thighs in offering, and I lean forward to take him into my mouth. I draw him in, and he strokes my cheek reverently.

"Good girl, my Bella. That's such a good girl."

I work him over for a long time. Until my knees are on fire from the pain and I'm certain he's about to come. But he stops me before I can get him there.

He grips me by the hair and leans down to meet my lips. Kissing me in a way that he never has before. Like he is worshipping me. Like he is tasting me for the first time. It goes on until I am dizzy. And then he instructs me to lay back.

I do.

My knees are grateful for the reprieve, but my back smarts when the tiny grains of rice dig into my flesh. The pain is soon forgotten as Javi kneels down before me and squeezes my thighs in his palms. He buries his face between my legs, and his tongue inside of me.

I cry out and jolt against him. He presses his palm into my stomach, holding me in place while he pleasures me.

I come hard.

And then I reach down and touch his face. I beg him for more. I plead for him. Javi leans back and drags me closer. His knees digging into the rice as he drives inside of me in one solid stroke.

He squeezes my hips and angles them for his pleasure, thrusting in and out of me with violent need. Grunting and slapping against me as he stares into my eyes.

It goes on forever. Until he can't hold himself up anymore. Until my body is completely limp in his arms. Until he finally roars out his release and then collapses beside me.

We lay there for a long time. Catching our breaths. Entranced by each other. I can feel that shift again. A barrier being swept away. It's liberating. It feels like progress. We have come so far together, extricating ourselves from the prisons of our hearts.

He kisses me again, and it's sweet.

Then he lifts me into his arms and sets me down on the chair, brushing the grains of rice from my skin and kissing the swollen flesh with his lips.

"Such a good girl, my Bella," he tells me again. "Would you like your reward now?"

I nod because it does not feel like a trick. Javi dresses himself. And then me. He retrieves a remote and turns on a projector I never knew existed in this room.

Fear twists in my stomach, but one look from him quickly snuffs it out. This is not a trick. Not this time. He brings me into his arms, turning me to face the screen. When it comes to life, I am surprised by what I see there.

A YouTube video. Of me. Singing at the piano. In Javi's house. Here at Moldavia.

Nobody else would know it, but I do. The room is black. So black. And I am playing one of my new songs. One that I sang for him. One that I wrote about him.

The video is public, for all the world to see. My chest squeezes as he scrolls through the comments. I'm expecting the worst.

I close my eyes and try to turn into him, but he guides my face back towards the screen and whispers in my ear.

"Open your eyes, Bella. This is your reward."

I open my eyes. And I read. The comments are not what I expected. They are positive. Uplifting. The listeners say how much they like the song. How they miss my voice. How they hope that I will put out more.

And there is more of the same, the longer Javi scrolls. I don't know how it's possible, but it is.

"You uploaded this?"

"Yes," he answers. "They miss you, Bella. It is not fair for me to keep your voice only to myself."

I turn to him, and this time, he lets me. And he does something else.

He wraps his arms around me and presses my cheek to his chest. And then he dances with me. Humming along to the music that I made. Music that I didn't even realize he recorded.

I wrap my arms around his waist, and I relax in his arms. For five minutes, nothing else outside of this room exists. For five minutes, Javi lets me inside. And in those five minutes, my emotions become so clear.

I am in love with my captor. He is my tormentor. My greatest source of pain and fear. But somehow, he has also become my sanctuary.

My whole world.

Chapter 33

Javier

Bella is in my bed.

The same place she has been every night for the last three weeks. She came to me on her own, and I could not bring myself to ask her to leave.

Even though I know it makes me weak. Even though I still question at times if it's real, or if she is even more skilled than her father at trickery.

She continues to come here, night after night. Curling her body into mine and wrapping my arm around her. She wakes in the morning and cooks breakfast, humming pieces of new music every day.

She seems happy. And this was not the way it was meant to go. This was not the way at all.

But when she kisses me this morning and looks up at me with sleepy eyes, I think that perhaps I never really stood a chance as far as Bella was concerned.

I think of Ray, and he seems like a distant memory now. My Bella does not speak of him. And I often wonder if she thinks of him. If she misses him, still. If it's true, she doesn't say.

Each night, I go to bed with a new resolve. That tomorrow, I will punish her. That tomorrow I will make her pay. But each dawn, my resolve is gone all over again.

My pulse hammers in my throat when she looks upon me. When she touches my scars and does not recoil. When she begs me to fuck her.

I do not know what she is doing to me. She is poisoning my mind. Ruining my plans. Making me forget my revenge. I should be furious with her for doing this. But instead, the contempt I feel is for myself.

I know that it cannot last. I know that my own mind is playing tricks on me. That given a choice, Bella would leave me. Because I have conditioned her to be this way.

It is an illusion. A temporary illusion. And in time, the spell she is under will fade away, leaving only her bitterness and her own desire for revenge.

If we continue down this path, I would let her take it. I would let her take my life to satisfy the inevitable darkness that lies buried in her heart beneath the lies. Because Bella cannot ever truly care for me. That was not the way this story began, and there's no changing that now.

She is a weakness. One that only metastasizes over time. And this is why I must act now. Before it is too late.

Today, I decide, is the day.

There is no other choice. I can no longer give in to the temptation of her. Which is why I climb from the bed before she can say a word. Before she can touch my lips, or ask me sweetly to be inside of her.

I tell her there is something I must do before I dress and leave the room.

I wait in my office until she is up and about, moving around the kitchen. And then I text River my instructions. When his reply comes through, I retrieve my toolbox and move to the entryway.

The window is stiff, and it must be pried from the place it has rested for so many years. It groans loudly, and I do not have to look to see if she is watching.

I can feel her eyes on me. Curious. I can almost hear the questions in her mind. And it is exactly what I wanted. So I do not know why I feel so ill. I do not know why I hesitate to answer when River's call comes through exactly as I asked.

I want to look at her. I want to see her one last time. But I don't. Because I know it will only make me change my mind. It will only make me weak.

With a stiff greeting, I answer River's call. He mumbles into the other line, asking me what's up. I tell him to hold on. I shut the window, but I do not lock it.

Bella is watching. Thinking I've become complacent. That I am comfortable. Perhaps even forgetful. Silently rejoicing as I walk to my office and close the door.

I ask River to give me an update on his end of the search for Ray so that I can use the time to think. To listen quietly to the sounds outside the room.

I can't bring myself to check the camera. Watching her come to terms with her decision before she slips away. I can't watch her leaving me because I will chase after her. I will want to punish her and lock her away again.

But I can't. It has to be now. I have to let her go. So she can no longer poison my mind. My heart.

"Javi," River says from the other end of the line.

"What?"

"You aren't listening to me. What is going on over there?"

"Nothing," I tell him. "It's nothing."

Silence greets me on the other end of the line. A long, painful silence. I know it will not last, and it doesn't.

"I knew this would happen."

"What would happen?" I ask.

"This girl," River snarls. "She has made you weak, Javier. She has poisoned you. Crippled you."

"No."

I don't sound convincing even to myself. And I do not deny what he says next either.

"Have you have fallen for her?"

The quiet is tense, and I do not possess the energy to argue with River right now. I can only think of my Bella. My Bella slipping further and further away from me.

It will take her twenty minutes to get to the main road. And from there, only a few minutes to the nearest gas station. She could be back home by noon.

"She does not love you, Javier," River tells me. "You must know she does not love you. It isn't real, whatever she thinks she feels. Whatever tricks she plays on you. They are the same we have been taught ourselves many times. You must know this."

"I am aware of that," I reply.

"And what of your revenge then?" he asks.

"My revenge will still be had. The past cannot be changed. I have damaged her, just as I set out to. I have tainted her. And when Ray comes home, he will see for himself."

"She does not look so damaged to me," River remarks. "Walking around your home as she pleases. Wearing clothing and doing whatever she feels like. You have gone soft."

It is true, so I do not dishonor him by telling him otherwise. But I do try to reassure him.

"It is done. It has already been done."

He is silent again, for several moments. Taking his time to gather the right words as River sometimes does.

"Do you remember how they tricked us?"

The memory of his fake murder still plays on repeat in my head. Every day, it has haunted me. The way they deceived me. The way they used River as a tool in my training.

They took everything from me.

I believed he was dead, for so many years. For so long, I had nothing else but the thought of my revenge. And River knows this too well.

"You were my only friend," he tells me. "My first friend. Do you remember that, Javi?"

"How could I ever forget?"

"They took you away from me," River says. "Ray took you away from me."

"I know."

"They tortured you too, Jav. Brainwashed you."

"I know," I say again.

"But what is the worst of his offenses?" he asks.

I do not answer. Because I do not have to. River already knows.

"Ray lied to you. He told you he believed you. But they chose you specifically, Jav. They turned you into a killer because they believed you were predisposed already. He tarred you with that brush, and he didn't care if it was true or not. He made you what you are. He destroyed you."

I close my eyes, and Bella seems so far away.

The rage is frothing inside of me, and River won't stop.

"They printed it right in your file, Jav. Those vile words about your mother. Have you forgotten so easily?"

The flashbacks wrench me back in time, swallowing me whole.

"Enough," I say.

But River does not listen. He speaks of my training with a level of detail that nobody else can. Because he is the only one who knows of my confessions. He speaks of the torture. The waterboarding. The burns. The mind games. The deceptions and punishments that followed.

He speaks of the blood I spilled. Repeatedly. The tests. And I tell him to stop, but he doesn't. He doesn't stop until I have smashed the phone against the wall and red is the only thing that I see.

Hatred. Rage. Hell.

The door crashes against the wall from the force of my adrenaline. The vein in my neck throbs and my footsteps ricochet down the hall as I stalk towards the kitchen.

She will be gone. She needs to be gone.

I wait for the cool air. The air that will inevitably linger from the window where she has escaped. The breeze that will carry her scent as she runs fast and far away from this place. From me.

I expect quiet. The peace that I desire so badly. But I do not find those things. Instead, I find my Bella, still at the kitchen stove, her eyes wide as she watches me come down the hall.

"Javi?" she whispers.

"Why are you still here?" I roar.

She backs into the counter and hugs herself, shaking her head frantically, but no words leave her mouth.

"You should have left when you had the chance!" I sneer.

I chase her around the counter and grab her arm, and she pleads with me as I drag her from the room.

"Javi, please. No, please. Whatever just happened, don't do this. I'm begging you."

Her words fall on deaf ears. I block out everything around me and focus on the red. The pain. The revenge.

I am no longer weak. Nothing can break me. Not even this girl and her trickery. This is what I tell myself. This is what I believe. Until she speaks again.

"Javi," she whispers. "Javi. I love you. Please. I love you."

I freeze. And I stare at her. This girl with the pale blue eyes, more venomous than even her father as she spills such lies from her lips.

I tell her so, and she tries to deny it.

"It's true," she says.

Tears track down her cheeks. And this time they do not make me weak. They do not make me want to fuck her either. They fill me with wrath all over again.

"You are a liar and a fool," I tell her.

"I am not a liar," she cries. "I may be many things, Javi. But a liar is not one of them. I will prove it to you. I'll do anything. Anything. Just tell me."

This time, I smile. And I feel like my old self again.

"Anything?" I ask.

"Anything," she replies.

Chapter 34

Isabella

Javi tugs me down the hall.

In a matter of seconds, everything has shifted. He is dragging me back to the past. Back to the room of horrors. The room where his mother carved him up. Where he carved me up. Where everything is bad between us and nothing is good.

This isn't where I want to go. But he asked me to prove myself. And I will. I will prove that it doesn't matter what he does to me.

He will see.

In the end, he will see that I am truthful. That I do love him. And my love for him is stronger than his rage. Stronger than his hurt and his fear and his vulnerability. I will break through those barriers if it's the last thing I do.

So when he straps me down to the table, I do not resist. I remain silent, even as he stuffs my mouth with another gag and takes away every last shred of free will that remains in me.

I do not cry. Even when he leaves the room. I do not feel ashamed when he comes to me the next morning and fucks my mouth and comes on my face.

I do not feel dirty when he comes back again at night and fucks me in the ass and comes on me again. I do not resist when he makes me pee in front of him and then restrains me once more.

I do not protest that my stomach is hungry and I have not eaten or showered. And I do not feel sorry that he has turned me into a feral animal all over again. Coming and going as he pleases throughout the day, using me like a toy. Covering me in his come and then leaving it to dry. Calling me names while he fucks me. Lashing out and insisting that I will tell the truth soon enough. That I will break.

But he is wrong. And it infuriates him that he is wrong. Because I do not break. Not even by the fourth day when I am truly disgusting.

He does not fuck me again on this fourth day. Instead, he releases me and tells me to go clean myself up.

He is too calm. Too silent. And I know something is not right. I expect the worst, the entire time I'm in the shower, scrubbing myself clean. Even when he tells me to get something to eat, I cannot. It only compounds my fear.

He goes back to his office. The house is too quiet. But the storm that's brewing is loud. I can feel it. I can feel it in my bones. Something awful is about to happen.

I saw it in his eyes.

The chill. The conviction. He intends to break me. Just as he always said he would do. He said he would destroy me. It's what he set out to do. And perhaps I have been a fool to think that he has changed, even after everything. Perhaps I am the only one who feels.

I don't have to wonder long. Because at nightfall, the bell on the door chimes again.

I expect River. It's always River. Never anyone else. Nobody else comes to Moldavia.

Nobody.

But it is not River at the door tonight. The scent of her perfume assaults me first. And then I see her in all her beauty, standing coyly on the threshold when Javi greets her.

This place is familiar to this woman. Javi is familiar to this woman. There is no doubt, she has had him before.

He gestures her inside, and I rot on the inside. Agony paralyzes me as he leads her down the hall to his bedroom. There is no second thought about me.

The door shuts with a resounding noise. My gut churns. My heart shrivels up and dies. And I was wrong. So, so wrong. Because Javi can still break me. He can still destroy me. He's done exactly that.

At first, I am immobile. Unable to move or blink or even breathe. And then the restlessness takes over.

I pace back and forth in the kitchen, frantic. Sick. My fingers quake and my head spins. I want to vomit. I want to scream. There are no tears. There is no sadness. I am captive to only one thing now.

Undiluted rage.

Hatred that burns so bright, I fear it will never be extinguished again. I can't control it. I can't deny it. The animal in me has taken the wheel.

The animal in me is the one who grabs a knife from the wooden block on the counter. The animal in me is the one who walks down the corridor and heaves open his bedroom door, expecting the worst. Poised to kill. Poised to kill them both.

But the woman in me sees only Javi, resting in a chair by the fire with a glass of whiskey in hand.

My eyes scan the room, seeking to destroy. But she is not here. She is not anywhere. The animal doesn't care. She wants retribution, and she will have it.

When Javi dares to look at me, I lunge for him, striking out at his chest. He grabs hold of my arm and halts the blade mid-swing.

"What's the matter, pet?" he taunts.

"I hate you!" I scream.

I try to thrust the knife again. This time he doesn't stop me, and it glances off his chest.

He's bleeding.

But it isn't enough. Not when I see the cruel laughter in his eyes. The way he mocks me with his lips.

"I thought you loved me," he sneers. "That's what you said. You said you would do anything. Anything to prove it."

"Not that," I cry.

And the tears are real now. Pain. So much pain. I feel like I've been punched in the heart.

"Where is she?" I demand. "Who is she?"

Javi snatches me by the throat and looks deep into my eyes. There was a time when my tears turned him on. A time when he liked to collect them like sweet memories. But now, they disgust him.

I disgust him. With my feelings and my humanity and my love.

"You never loved me," he snarls.

"Fuck you," I choke out.

He smiles. And it scares me more than any of his other smiles. Because there is nothing behind it. He is dead. He is without anything now.

I don't know how it came to this. How everything changed so abruptly. Even as he drags me to the bed and tears off my clothes, I want to believe that there is hope. I want to believe all is not lost.

This is just another temporary bout of insanity. But I should know by now. Everything Javi does leaves a permanent scar.

He unbuttons his jeans and thrusts inside of me without warning.

"Fucking liar," he chants.

"You're the liar!" I scream. "You're pathetic. You can't even admit your own feelings. You can't even admit that you care for me."

It's the wrong thing to say.

He stops. And dread fills my stomach. I try to look back at him, but he presses my face into the bed. Then he takes his cock out and nudges it against my ass.

I bite my lip to keep from crying out when he shoves inside. Now he wants my tears for a whole different reason. To punish me. But I won't give him the satisfaction. I won't let him see my pain. Not anymore.

My strength only enrages him further as he grabs me by the hair and yanks.

"You are nothing," he tells me. "Nothing!"

To further prove his point, he reaches for a pillow and frees it from the case. And then he wraps the case over my head, so he doesn't have to look at me.

He fucks me raw. Hard. Brutal. Neither one of us says a word.

I cry silent tears behind the veil of the pillowcase, and he grunts out his frustrations before finishing inside of me. And when he is done, he pushes me away with one final parting blow.

"Nothing."

Chapter 35

Javier

When I wake, it is to the sound of the private phone line ringing.

River.

A glance at the clock confirms that it is three am, and I fell asleep at my desk. Drunk. I'm still drunk when I pick up the phone, and his words are not clear. That is my initial reaction.

"Ray is back," I hear.

"What?"

My head throbs and my eyes burn.

"Check your email."

I rouse my computer from slumber. My inbox is filled with alerts.

> *Ray Rossi has been found.*
> *Alive.*

My initial reaction should be relief. This is what I've been waiting for. Hoping for. The day has finally come. Ray is alive. And he will finally know the suffering I have inflicted upon his daughter.

Upon Bella.

River mumbles something from the other line, asking if I'm still there. I disconnect the call and stare at the screen.

My gut churns. It's too soon. That's my only thought. It's too soon. I wasn't ready for this. I'm not ready to let her go. I tell myself that she hasn't been broken. That I need more time.

But it's a lie.

Because it does not matter what I did before. Nothing else matters. After tonight, she will never look at me the same way again. My Bella is as broken as broken can get.

She has seen me for what I am. She has seen me at my worst. She has dared to hope. And her hope has turned to dust.

I flip over to the house security screens and search for her in the dim light. She is not in my room. Or the conservatory. Or even her own room.

I continue searching, and I do not find her in the piano room. Or the library. Or the kitchen. Or any room. Dread coils deep inside as I search them one by one again.

Something is wrong. Something is off. She isn't anywhere.

I leave my office and check the only places without cameras. The bathrooms. But they are empty too. I pace the halls and check the doors and windows.

All locked.

I can find no trace of her. Not one. My mind conjures up the worst scenarios as I retrace her last steps.

My bedroom is the same as I left it. The pillowcase is now on the floor, next to her panties. And her shoes.

Her shoes.

Next to the bed, the floor board is misplaced.

The trap door. The same trap door I sent the prostitute through upon her arrival this evening. And I don't know how I missed it. How I could have been so careless.

My Bella is so smart. So observant. It is too late. I fear it is too late. I have lost her forever.

Following her scent, I descend into the passageway and find my way along the walls in the darkness. Waiting for a sound. A shadow. But there are none.

When I reach the end, my worries are only compounded. The door is cracked, a sliver of moonlight spilling in from the outside. This is the way she left.

It's almost four am now. I don't know how long she has been out here. I don't know if she found her way in the darkness. Flagged down a passing car on the old dirt road.

What if someone took her? Someone worse than me?

My chest caves in. There is nobody worse than me. That's what I'd like to believe. But for my Bella, there are others who could be worse. I have to find her. I have to get to her and...

There is a footprint in the dirt.

It's not right. She went the wrong way. She came out in the darkness and could not see the path to the road, so she unknowingly ventured deeper into the forest instead.

I walk beside her footprints and retrace her steps. They are wild at first. She was running. But as the brush thickens, the footsteps disappear, and I have only broken twigs and bent leaves to rely on.

I listen for her. My eyes seek out her hair, shining in the moonlight. I do not see it. Not after ten minutes. Not even after thirty. But the trail is still here. And so I keep going. I keep searching, hoping that my Bella is still here.

After two hours, I still have not found her. And all traces of her disappear abruptly. There is nothing. But I am in the middle of the forest. It doesn't make sense.

I stop, and I listen. And eventually, I hear something. The faintest of sobs from behind a tree.

I find her curled into herself, her face resting on her knees. She does not look up, even though she knows I'm here. She continues to cry. Shattered. Defeated.

Her feet are bloody, and her knees are skinned. She is scratched from head to toe.

I scoop her up into my arms, and she does not fight me. She does not say a word the entire walk back to the house. She does not say a word as I draw her a bath and clean her wounds. She remains silent even as I bandage her. It is only when I put her to bed that she looks up at me.

Broken.

Empty.

Her eyes are absent of the light that used to shine so bright.

"I was wrong," she whispers.

"Wrong about what, Bella?"

"I don't love you," she tells me. "I despise you."

I swallow. And I wish I had just let her stab me. But I give her the words that she needs to hear now. The only ones that matter.

"Then your transformation is complete. And nobody can ever hurt you again, my sweet."

Chapter 36

Isabella

My bones are weary and everything aches, right down to my very soul.

Javi lays me in bed. His bed. If I had any energy left to argue, I still don't know that I could.

I certainly don't have any fight left when he lies beside me and swallows me in his arms. He holds me while I cry. Comforting the hurt that he caused. The despair that is so much a part of me now I doubt I'll ever be right again.

I think that Javi is correct. He has broken me completely this time.

He thinks I can protect myself now. But I've never been able to protect myself from him. Because even as we lay here in the solace of darkness, unburdened from the heavy strain that still lives between us in the light- his presence does comfort me.

I bury my face into his chest and breathe him in. I beg him to stop. What, I don't know. I just want it to stop. I want it all to go away.

Either let the blackness swallow me whole, or push me back into the light. It's too much. Too much to be torn between the two.

He holds me closer still and tells me it will all be over soon. Then he kisses me. He kisses me like it's the last time he will ever kiss me. And we fall asleep.

Together.

***

I wake with a sluggish heartbeat and an invisible pressure bearing down on me. I don't know where it came from, this foreboding feeling inside of me. Because when I open my eyes, Javi is still there. Watching me silently as he strokes my arm.

Desolation shadows his eyes, and I think it is only fair. I wonder if he slept at all, and then I remind myself that I don't care. Because I hate him.

We all lie to ourselves, sometimes.

His scars are unsheltered in the early morning light. Old and new, they litter his body in shades of pink and white. Today, my monster is visibly fraught with sorrow.

This battle has raged within him for so long. Whatever torture Javi suffered, it extended far beyond his body. It embedded itself within his mind and made a home there.

He's been caught between two sides, just as I have.

Only now, he's made his decision. It's written in his eyes. What's done is done. But I don't have a map to his secret language, and I am too weary to guess anymore. Whatever my fate is, it's for the gods or Javi to decide.

He pets my cheek and brushes his lips against my forehead. Gentle. Sweet. Reverent. It terrifies me. It soothes me. And I cry when I reach out to touch him.

I'm in too much pain to move. Javi does not smile this time. He does not exalt in this kind of pain. Instead, he tells me to hold tight while he retrieves some pills and a glass of water. He helps me to sit up and waits until I have swallowed them before he lays me back down.

The distance between us now may as well be an ocean. He remains on the edge of the bed. His thoughts are somewhere else.

"What is it, Javi?" I ask him. "What's happening?"

His eyes move over me, and they are open now. Mournful and reverent.

"I was only thinking that perhaps I would like to be selfish," he says.

"I don't understand what you mean."

His lip curls up at the corner in the faintest hint of a smile.

"I think you have made me want to keep you. And that would be the most selfish thing of all, my Bella."

I don't want to hope. I don't want to fall for any more of his cruel deceptions. I can't afford to get stung again. Not when I am so empty. But it does not feel like a trick anymore. Not with his eyes on me like this. Not with his voice gentle and sad and thoughtful.

"You said you would always keep me," I remind him. "Always."

I don't want him to throw me away. Maybe that makes me pathetic. Maybe it makes me so fucked up in the head I can't be fixed. But when he even mentions a scenario where we don't exist together, I can't cope. The possibility douses me in fresh terror.

Javi is the poison I drink so willingly because nothing else has ever tasted so sweet.

He is everything. The light and the dark. The solace and the pain. The torment and the peace. And I can't imagine not having him here with me. I can't even consider it.

My nails dig into the flesh of my palms until I draw blood.

"You promised," I tell him again. "You promised that you would keep me forever."

"My Bella." He comes back to me, tilting my chin so that his lips hover over mine. "It is alright. I am here now, yes?"

I buckle in his arms, and he catches me. His touch hurts like nothing else ever has.

It is the best kind of pain. The only pain I ever want. Javi drags his nose down my throat, breathing me in.

"Say what you said before," he whispers. "Say it, and this time, I will try to believe it."

It scares me. It scares me so much I hold onto him so he can't let me go. But I say the words. I tell him the irrefutable truth in our bed of lies.

"I love you, Javi. I love you so much. You've fucked me up so bad. You've messed with my head, and I don't know... there are so many things I don't know. I don't know how to fix them. Or unbreak them. But this is the one thing I know. I love you."

He does not lash out this time. He holds me. He kisses me.

Whispered apologies flow from his lips over and over. He tells me everything is going to be alright. He says he will protect me and never let me go.

For once, my mind and my heart are at peace. There is light in the darkness.

And I believe him.

Chapter 37

Isabella

Javi tries to rouse me from my sleep, and I dig in deeper. My dreams are too sweet, and his touch is so warm against me.

I don't want to move. I don't want to go anywhere other than this space between my dream and reality. But he is insistent.

"My Bella, I need you to wake up. Wake up and be a good girl for me, yes?"

My eyes are cemented together, and the thing that he asks of me is easier said than done. The pills he gave me knocked me out. I don't know how long it's been.

Days, months, weeks.

I'm groggy and confused when I realize that I'm already dressed. Not just dressed. But dressed for outside, with a coat and shoes and socks. My hair is braided too.

I blink up at him, and he is still blurry until my eyes adjust to the light.

"It is time to go," he tells me. "There is something we must do together."

I shake my head and tell him no. Whatever it is, I don't want to go.

"You will want to see this, my Bella."

Still, I try to pull the blankets back over me. Javi sighs.

"It is about your father."

And now he has my attention.

"What about him?"

My voice is froggy. I sound weird. Terrified. Terrified that he will have bad news for me. But Javi's only answer is to help me from the bed.

"Come," he insists.

I follow him. It isn't easy. I'm still in pain. But he helps me every step of the way, allowing me to lean on him for support.

He unlocks the front door, and my legs grow weak before locking into place. I don't want to leave anymore. I only want to stay.

The caged bird is me.

And I am afraid. More afraid than I have ever been in my whole life to step foot out that door. But I know that I must. Whatever news there is of my father, I must go. I must find out.

Knowing and doing are two different things. So even when Javi steps outside, I hesitate on the threshold. He looks back at me, extending his hand. A gesture that means so much more than just this moment.

It's there in his eyes. The change I had been hoping for all along. His barriers down. My monster is asking me to walk beside him. To trust him to guide me. To protect me and care for me.

With this knowledge, I step beside him. He holds my hand and nods. He feels it too. We are in this together. The walls have come down, and the only barriers we have now are those of the outside world.

He leads me to a motorcycle. His only mode of transportation. After providing me with a helmet, he helps me onto the back and secures my arms around his waist.

The engine roars to life, and the comfort of his scent surrounds me when I lean into his back. He drives us away from Moldavia and back towards the lights of the city.

My heart is calm, but my mind is loud with questions. It only gets louder when the scenery begins to change. When Javi turns into my old neighborhood. Then onto my street.

I hold onto him long after he parks in the driveway. He doesn't move either. But then the front door opens. And everything implodes.

My father stands on the stoop. The same stoop where I never thought I would see him again.

He is alive.

And his eyes are on me. Swimming with relief. I try to spring from the bike, but Javi captures me around the wrist. Our eyes meet for a split second, and there is real fear in his. Fear that he might lose me.

"Javi, it's okay," I tell him. "It's okay."

He hesitates for another long second before releasing me. I bound towards the stoop, the aches in my body fleeing in the presence of the joy I feel at this moment.

My father moves to meet me. Slower than usual. He is walking with a limp. But he is alive. Alive and... hugging me.

I sob against his chest. There are no words. None. Not between either of us, for a very long time. We just hold each other. And I am a little girl all over again. But he has never held me this way.

It feels so right. It feels like everything in my world is right again. Until I look up at his face and catch the way he is staring at Javi.

I have never seen him look at anyone this way. I have never seen so much hate. My arms fall away, and I wrap them around myself instead.

Relief dissipates and fades into confusion. Turmoil. The reality of my current situation is like a brick to the face. There is no peace to be had. There never was. Because now I'm caught between the two of them. The two men that I love the most.

The two men who hate each other.

"Let's go inside," Dad says. "Shall we?"

Javi dismounts from his bike and reaches the stoop in three long strides. Both men try to usher me in beside them, but Javi is the one I allow to guide me.

I don't know why.

I am ashamed when I see the hurt in my father's eyes. I am torn. I want to feel happy, but right now, all I feel is that the ground is about to give way beneath me at any moment. And Javi is the one I lean to.

He has been my source of comfort and pain for so long now. Perhaps it is just conditioning, but it doesn't make it less real. I want my father to understand that. But it is clear he does not.

I try to read the unspoken messages that linger between them. Awful silence fills the room as they look to each other and then me.

Dad instructs us to take a seat on the couch while he sits in his usual chair. The chair that has been empty for so long.

I have so many questions.

"Where have you been?" I ask.

And now it is me who is unable to hide the hurt. It might not be rational, and I never realized it until now, but a part of me has blamed him for his absence. A part of me has been so angry with him for leaving me.

"Isa, I am so sorry," he answers. "Something went bad on a job. It wasn't meant to happen this way, but it did, and I'm sorry for the pain I have caused you."

"That isn't good enough," I tell him, swiping away the fresh wave of tears as they fall. "You've been gone for months. I need to know where. I can't accept your canned responses anymore. I need to know what happened to take you away."

He sighs and rubs his forehead.

"I was in South America," he says. "Our convoy got hit by a rebel group, and they took us hostage."

I search his eyes, trying to discern whether he is telling me the truth. But the reality is, I don't know. I have always accepted whatever my father told me without question. Only now, I am not so sure.

Regardless, it doesn't matter where he was. He could tell me whatever he wanted to, and I wouldn't know the difference. He could be spoon feeding me agency scripted dialogue, for all I know.

The important thing is that he's home. And he's safe. This is what I try to tell myself.

"There is much to discuss, my dearest Isabella," he continues on. "But we have all the time in the world for that. First, I must know. Are you okay?"

He glances at Javi again as he asks.

I swallow and nod. It doesn't look natural, but I really do feel okay. Dad isn't buying what I'm selling either though. His eyes are roaming over my scratched face and arms.

"They are nothing," I assure him. "I'm okay, Dad. I promise. I'm just so happy to have you home. I thought… I thought I would never see you again."

My voice cracks and he reaches out to take my hand in his, squeezing with reassurance.

"I am okay, Isa," he assures me too. "I promise."

I choke back my emotion to give him a watery smile. Beside me, Javi squeezes my other hand. A gesture of comfort and possession. I glance at him and smile too. He wraps his hand around my knee, staking his claim on me in a way that provokes my father even further.

"Isa," my father commands. "I would like to speak to Javi alone."

Javi sneers, and he does not break eye contact from my father when he tells me it's okay. I rise to give myself distance from both of them.

"No."

"No?" they both ask in unison.

"I said no," I reiterate. "I'm done with the secrets. With the lies. Whatever has happened between you, I deserve to know the truth. The whole truth. And I'm not going anywhere until I do."

My father shifts in his chair, unbuttoning the top of his shirt and rubbing at his throat. Javi is still calm, but now his eyes are on me. Concerned. I don't like it. But it only makes my point that much more valid.

My father does not miss Javi's concern, and he seems to relax if only a little.

"Would you like to start, Javier?"

Javi scoffs at him and then paces the length of the floor.

"You would like that," he says. "You would like me to be the one to hurt her this way. Because you are a coward."

My father does not answer. His easiness is gone now, and all that remains is the flint in his eyes. Neither one of them is backing down from this silent war of wills. Javi moves towards me and tucks me back into his side.

"This is where we stand," Javi says. "Bella has been with me for the duration of your long absence. Much has changed since you were gone. Because she has been with me, and she has fallen in love with me."

The guardianship in his tone and body language can't be denied. Even his stance is fierce. Protective. For some reason, he feels the need to safeguard me from my own father. But his eyes are soft and warm when he looks in my direction.

"And I have fallen for her, as well."

My father shakes his head in disgust, but I can only focus on Javi's words.

He just admitted that he's in love with me. In front of my father. I don't know what this means. But my stomach won't stop fluttering, and my head is all fuzzy. I'm smiling, and I can't help it.

Even though my father's face is tomato red. Even though he looks so disappointed in me right now. He curses in Italian and scrapes a hand through his balding hair.

"I suppose you feel as though you have served your just desserts then."

"I will not deny that it is precisely what I set out to do with Bella," Javi admits with shame in his eyes.

"It doesn't matter," I tell them both. "None of that matters now. It's the past. Dad, you are back home now. And Javi and I... we love each other."

"What have you done to my little girl?" My father howls.

His eyes are teary when he looks at me, pleading.

"Isa, he is a dangerous man. Whatever he has done to you... we can get you help. Whatever you think you are feeling for him right now, it isn't real."

Javi argues before I can, speaking in his native Spanish tongue, which my father understands but I do not. My head hurts as they continue to bicker, and I realize that maybe this wasn't the best idea after all.

I can't understand their words. But body language has no barrier. They hate each other. It is clear as day.

I still don't understand what happened between them. But despite the obvious tension in the room, I'm on a cloud of euphoria right now. It feels as though the storm clouds have finally lifted away and the sun is shining again.

Javi loves me. And my father has returned. The rest will have to work itself out. The rest, we can figure out later.

My father segues back to English, and Javi follows suit, answering him so that I can hear.

"I have hurt her," Javi says. "As I set out to do."

The tone of his voice threatens my haze of blissful ignorance. Something is off. Something is wrong. Javi is withdrawn. His eyebrows pinched, his shoulders tense.

He looks so ashamed. So guilty. And worse, he looks so far away.

"I learned from the best," he continues. "I had every intention of coming here to thank you, Ray. For guiding me. For showing me the way. For teaching me how to destroy the fragile minds of people who are not like us."

My father's face pales, and a cold sweat forms over my body. I don't know what he's saying. That my father did this to him? That he did to Javi, what Javi did to me?

I look up at Javi and see nothing but genuine sincerity on his face. He reaches out to touch my face, and for a moment, I forget everything else and focus on him. On the light in my heart. The one I thought long since extinguished, which now burns bright.

"My Bella," he whispers. "I wanted to be selfish. I would give anything to be selfish if I did not know that there was only one possible outcome from all of this."

My heart stops beating. My lungs stop taking in air. And I'm shaking my head before he can even say it.

"What do you mean?"

"Isa."

My father's voice is harsh. Harsher than it's ever been with me, and he's looking at me like he doesn't know me at all right now. Like I am no longer his daughter, standing here in the house that I grew up in.

"What Javi is trying to say is that the things you are feeling right now, they aren't real. And in time you will see that. You will understand that when you've had some time to heal. To contemplate the reality of your situation."

"No," I tell them both. "Don't try to tell me what I feel. I love Javi. And it's real. I will always love him."

My father sighs and Javi looks away. I don't like this. I don't like where this is going. I won't let him leave me behind, and I tell him so.

"I need a drink," my father says. "Will you get us a drink Isa, please."

His bar is still stacked against the wall where he left it, so I don't have to leave the room. It gives me the opportunity to clear my head. To digest everything that's happening.

I reach for the bourbon, and my father interrupts me.

"Not that," he says. "The Macallan."

I look back at him in question. He only drinks this whiskey on special occasions. But I guess today is a special occasion, being that he is alive.

I pour two glasses and take one to him and hand the other to Javi. They stare at each other from their seats, and I remain quiet between them.

My father swirls the amber liquid in his glass, staring into the abyss as he gathers his thoughts.

"This is over," he says to Javi. "I'll never allow it to continue."

I rub my temples and look at my father.

"It isn't up to you," I tell him. "Dad, please. Don't do this. Not today."

"You don't know what you are saying, Isa. You have been brainwashed."

Javi meets my father's gaze head on.

"And you have a right to speak about brainwashing?"

Dad's face is red and mottled all over again.

"There are many things you do not understand," he tells Javi. "That you never could. You want to believe only what you want to believe."

Javi looks at me and shakes his head, his eyes sad.

"Bella does not need to hear these things."

My father silently agrees, and the room falls still again. Too still. Like the calm before the storm. The tension is still there, simmering below the surface. And I am anxious now because I don't know when it's going to erupt. But I know one thing, and that is I won't let Javi leave without me.

Not today. Not ever.

They both stare over the rims of their glasses, like snakes poised to strike. Javi is the first to drink, swallowing the entire contents of the tumbler in one fell swoop.

And then he looks at me again. His face contorted. At first, I think he is angry with me. But then he coughs. And sputters. And coughs again.

"Javi?"

I move to his side, but he doesn't respond.

It all happens in horrific slow motion. The color drains from Javi's face while my father looks into his own tumbler and it shatters to the floor.

"Dad?" I scream.

Javi falls back against the sofa and begins to convulse.

"Dad! Help him. What's happening? Please help him."

My father rushes to Javi's side and begins chest compressions. I grab Javi's face, trying to see him. Trying to see his eyes, but they are closed, and he is lifeless.

It's all happening too fast.

It's all too real. Nothing about this makes sense. He was just talking to me. And now he's lying here, and I can't see his eyes. I can't feel his heartbeat or hear his breath.

I'm sobbing. Begging him not to go anywhere. Demanding that he stops this right now. He can't trick me anymore. He can't play these games with me anymore. I'm too fragile, and I can't survive it. Not this time. Not when he said he loved me, and I believed him.

During the chaos, the front door opens, and someone else appears. In the back of my mind, I hope that it's the ambulance. The ambulance that's coming to rescue him. To fix him. The ambulance that we haven't even had time to call. But paramedics don't wear a mask. And they don't have guns, either.

"Time to say goodbye, little Bella," the strange voice tells me.

"What?" I blink and cling to Javi. "No."

None of this is real. It can't be. It just can't. I don't know what's happening. Only that I'm sobbing hysterically and Javi isn't moving, and I'm so scared. My father keeps saying that he's sorry. He's so sorry. There's nothing he can do.

But he's a liar, and I hate him.

I hate him so much, and I can't even comprehend why at this moment. He's dragging me away from Javi.

The masked men are shouting orders. But I can't hear them. Because I'm trying to get to Javi. I'm trying to fight my father off. But he's too big. Too strong. And the men are taking Javi away from me. Dragging him out the front door.

I scream at them to stop. Only one of them does, just to look back at me one last time.

"I will send you the ashes, little Bella. It's what he would have wanted."

Chapter 38

Isabella

Darkness.

It possesses me. It entombs me. And darkness is all that I am now. The void is empty and vast. It cannot be mended.

Nothing can ever be fixed again.

My father comes to my room often to check on me. The room where he has locked me. The room where he tries to feed me.

I have traded one prison for another.

He tells me he wants to keep me safe. He tells me he doesn't know who to trust. But when I look at his face, it is him I don't trust.

I trust nobody. I feel nothing. Nothing can hurt me anymore. It's what Javi wanted. And I refuse to believe that this is my reality. I refuse to believe that he isn't here with me.

I'm back in the piano room. Everything else is an invention of my imagination. My hallucination. That's what I keep telling myself. That's how I go on, breathing and thinking and living.

He's going to come for me soon. He will tell me that it's all been a trick. And now it's time for my reward. Because I've been a good girl for him, he will comfort me. He will take me in his arms and hold me. Fix me. Give me the thing only he can provide.

My sanctuary.

My peace.

"Isa," my father's voice echoes through the cavernous space of my new prison. "You must eat. You must stay healthy and strong."

I blink up at his distorted face, and I am glad that he is obscured. I can't bear to meet the eyes of this man who has raised me.

This man who- in my nightmare- took Javi away from me.

It plays on in my head. Over and over again. The whiskey. The whiskey he asked me to pour. The whiskey he did not drink. And the expression on Javi's face.

Betrayal.

It was the last thing I saw in his eyes. The last thing he felt in this nightmare. He thought I had betrayed him. My stomach churns, and I curl into myself. My cheeks are wet, but I know the tears don't mean anything.

It still isn't real.

Javi will come for me. He will ask me to play him a song with words only he can hear. I will play him a million songs. And I will sing words that I have never sung before.

When my father leaves, I scribble them down in my journal. I write pages upon pages of lyrics. Frantically. Endlessly. Until my hands are black with ink and my eyes are too blurry to see anymore.

"Sing me a song, Javi," I whisper into the darkness. "With words only I can hear."

I repeat it, over and over. I cry. I pace. I never sleep. I don't eat. I drink water only when my father makes me.

I'm dead inside already.

And the longer the days go on, the less certain I am. The harder it becomes to deny. He will come for me. That's what I tell myself. That's what I tell my father. Until the day that he comes for me instead. And he carries something with him this time.

It is a card. And something else.

A silver urn.

An urn painted with crimson roses.

"This came for you today."

His voice is solemn, and I hate him.

"No." I yank the urn from his arms and clutch it to my chest. "No!"

I scream. I scream it over and over.

"This is your fault! You did this to me!"

Tears fill his eyes, and he looks at the floor. I can't pretend anymore. Because I'm dead inside. There is nothing left in me.

Nothing.

And I know that Javi is really gone.

And I know that I'll never be okay again.

* * *

My room is small. Sterile. White. But the tiles are sea foam green. Like the horror room at Moldavia. I wonder if Javi noticed that too when he was here.

In the sanitarium.

My therapist sits across from me, observing the pattern my fingers trace over the urn that doesn't leave my side.

"Tell me what's on your mind, Isabella," she says.

I forgot her name. Or I don't care. Names aren't important anymore. Nothing is important anymore.

"I was wondering if this was his room," I tell her. "I was wondering if the bed that I sleep in was his too."

"And if it was, how would that make you feel?"

I look at her this time.

"It would make me feel happy."

But that's a lie. Nothing can make me happy anymore. Not when grief is the only thing that exists.

My father thinks I'm wrong. Disjointed. Mentally incapable of understanding my own thoughts. He thinks I have Stockholm syndrome. He says I've been brainwashed into hating him and loving Javi instead.

But he's wrong.

I hate them both. I hate my father for his lies. And I hate Javi for leaving me. For ever loving me. For making me love him. I tell the therapist so, and she doesn't judge me. At least not out loud.

"I hate them," I tell her again. My voice is rougher this time. "I hate them both."

"Anger is a normal part of grief," she replies.

I don't want her justifications. Her agreement. I don't know what I want. I've been here for two weeks, and nothing has changed. She can't fix me. Only Javi can.

But nobody understands that. They think I'm wrong for thinking so.

"Would you like to play the piano today, Isabella?"

I nod this time. Because I will play every day now. Every chance I get. I play him songs. But I don't sing the words out loud.

Because they are only for him. Words only he can hear.

The room is quiet, and the therapist is too. I don't like it when she's quiet. It's easier when she asks me questions. Otherwise, I say things. Things that I shouldn't say.

"He isn't bad," I tell her. "You don't know him."

"I never said he was," she answers.

Her voice is gentle, but I don't believe her.

"His mother did awful things to him. And then my father. Something happened to him. He was tortured."

She sits back and crosses her legs. Folding her hands over her lap as she watches me carefully.

"Why do you feel the need to validate, Isabella?"

"I see how you look at me," I answer. "I see how you all look at me. How you scribble your notes. How my father whispers to you when I can't hear. I know what you think. But you won't change my mind. You won't fix me. Or unbreak me. Or convince me that what I feel isn't real."

She sets her pen aside. Her notebook is empty today. And I'm glad.

"What if I said that I do believe you?" she asks. "What if I told you that what you feel is real? That your love for Javi is real. Would you believe me?"

I trace over the roses again.

"I don't think so."

"Then perhaps the person you are trying to convince is yourself."

Her words confuse me. They make my head hurt. I don't need to convince myself. I already know that my love for Javi is real.

"Do you feel guilt for loving him?" she continues. "Or is it guilt for his death?"

Death.

The word punches me in the gut all over again. I want to tell her to shut up. I want to tell her that he isn't dead. But he is.

He's right here beside me. And I'll never hold him again. I squeeze my eyes shut, and the only thing I can see is that look on his face.

The betrayal.

It's the only thing I see. Day and night. Every other memory has vanished, and this is all that remains. The haunting final moments when he was there, and then he wasn't.

"He thought I did it," I whisper. "He thought it was me. It was the last thing he thought."

Tears leak from my eyes and I feel weak for crying all the time.

The therapist doesn't say anything. She lets me cry. She lets me feel. And it hurts so much. I wish she would just give me some pills. To numb everything. To make it go away. But she hasn't given me any.

I ask her why, and she reaches for her pen again, tapping it against the corner of the desk.

"I can't give you any pills, Isabella."

"But why?" I ask her again. "Isn't that the whole point? The whole point of me being here?"

"The whole point of you being here is to rest," she replies. "To be well."

I ignore her and go back to tracing over the roses. She watches me. She is silent for a long time before she speaks again.

"I think you are strong, Isabella. I think you are brave. And I think Javi would want you to be well too. He would want you to be at peace."

"How can I be at peace?" I demand. "When he isn't here?"

She is quiet again. Her brow furrowed.

"What if I told you that a part of him was? What if I told you that you had another reason to be strong?"

Her words capture me. She knows it. But she does not explain right away. She watches me closely, gauging my reactions. And then when she has determined that I am ready to hear it, she goes on.

"Do you remember when your father brought you here? Do you remember the tests we ran that first day, Isabella?"

I nod. I was despondent then. I wouldn't answer their questions. I didn't need to. They took their answers from my father. From blood tests and eye tests and reflexes and other things that were supposed to measure how sick I was in the head.

The answers to those tests are in my chart. The chart she carries with her now. She opens it up and reaches inside, flipping through to the back. And then she pulls out a piece of paper, sliding it across the desk towards me.

"Isabella, the reason Javi still lives on is because he is here with you right now. Inside of you. You are pregnant with his child."

Chapter 39

Isabella

Moldavia is the same as it always was.

Shadowy. Secluded. Mysterious. But somehow, everything has changed.

Inside is dusty. Stagnant. A time capsule of our last moments together. Javi's bed is still unmade, where we slept together that night. The bandages remain on the bedside table, from when he mended me after I tried to escape. And the glass he brought me to take my pills remains, empty.

It is an ache unlike any other when I walk around this house. When I don't feel him here. I try to be strong. I try to remember everything I learned from my therapy. I want to hold on to the good memories and push forward. But it's hard when everything is so desolate around me.

It's hard when every time I have to breathe, it hurts.

His child grows inside of my belly. And I have to do this on my own. It cracks me open and makes me bleed all over again. But the worst pain comes when I visit the conservatory. When I see the roses have withered and died in his absence.

The once familiar scent that used to surround us no longer lives.

Even the house is in mourning. I can't feel him here. I don't feel him here at all. I have to see him one more time. In the only way I can.

I walk to the bathroom, and I find the makeup case. The one where I stashed the tapes. The tapes that have haunted me for so long.

I don't know what's on these.

I don't know why they were hidden away from the others. But I have nothing left to lose now. I have nothing left to fear. The worst has already happened. There can be nothing on these tapes that's worse than what I've already witnessed. That's what I tell myself as I walk to the projector.

They are numbered, so I start with the first. The projector sputters to life, but nothing plays on the screen. I try the next tape. And the next. And the next. They are all blank.

All along, they meant nothing.

There was nothing here. It doesn't make sense. Why were they locked away? I can't think about it anymore. I can't focus.

I put on one of his tee shirts, and I cry. But only for an hour. That's all I will allow myself. Because I have to keep moving forward. I have to, for my baby. For our baby.

I have to make a home. I have to play my music. I have to stay busy. And most importantly...

I have to plan a funeral.

* * *

My father comes to the door in the afternoon, his shoulders falling in relief when I answer it.

"Isa, I was so worried. You should not have run off like that."

"I'm an adult," I answer. "And I was free to go. I did not need your permission."

His eyes are sad when he looks at me. I am sad too. I don't know how it came to this. I don't know who this man is.

"I know what you did," I tell him.

"I did not kill him, Isa," he insists. "I know you find this difficult to understand, but I cared for Javi. I cared for him like a son. And I am mourning his death too..."

"I'm not talking about that."

Guilt washes over his face. He tugs at his collar, his mind silently formulating the next untruth.

"Don't lie to me," I bluff. "I've seen the tapes."

His reaction is small. But it's there. The slightest flash of worry darkens his eyes before he masks it again.

"Isa, I do not know what you are speaking of."

"Yes, you do. He was tortured. Because of you. You took him from one hell and sent him to another. He loved you. How could you do that to him?"

"I had no choice. Isa, you don't understand."

"I understand that you betrayed him. All those years, you told me I could never meet him. That he was dangerous. But in reality, he was only the monster you created."

"I was following orders," he says. "You don't understand how the agency works. If I had not followed those orders, I would be dead. And then what would become of you?"

"Then I would have at least known that my father was an honorable man."

My words cut him, and I can't hold back the emotion in my voice. The shame. The anger. The grief.

I want to take the words back as soon as I say them. I hate this. I hate being so conflicted. Living between love and hate. First with Javi. And now with my father.

"Isa," he pleads. "Forgive me. I'm so sorry."

He pulls me into his arms, and I don't fight this time. It hurts so much. I want to forgive him, but I don't know how I can. How can I when I still don't know the truth about Javi's death.

"Have you heard anything more about River?" I ask.

My father's arms stiffen around me, and I pull away.

"Tell me," I demand. "You have to tell me."

"Let me come inside," he implores.

I let him into the parlor and shut the door behind him. He gestures to the kitchen, and we take a seat at the counter. I don't offer him a drink. The time for pleasantries is over.

"There is much more to River than I knew," my father begins.

"Javi trusted him," I say. "He trusted him with his life. With my life. He thought he was his friend."

"I trusted him too," my father answers. "I didn't realize how deep this went."

"What do you mean?"

"River is employed by the agency."

I shake my head. That can't be right. Javi would have known.

"They've known each other since the sanitarium," I argue.

"I know," my father replies. "That's why his cover worked so well. He is a handler of sorts. That was his role all along. He was inserted into Javi's life at a young age to build a relationship of trust."

"But why?" I ask. "Why would they do that?"

"Because Javi was a valuable asset," he answers. "One that, in the right hands, could have been a dangerous weapon. If he ever decided to act on his own, to work for another agency, it could have devastated the entire house of cards."

"So, you're telling me the agency is behind his death? That doesn't make sense. Why would they hurt him?"

"I don't know."

I want to believe him, but I don't know that I can.

"I know River cared for him," my father tells me. "That wasn't a lie. I know he cared for him."

His words make no difference now. What does it matter if he cared when he disappeared without an explanation?

"I'm tired," I say. "I think I'm going to rest now."

He shakes his head, his eyes pleading with me.

"You can't stay here, Isa. It isn't safe. Not until we know what's going on."

"Nowhere is safe," I reply. "Not when I have no idea who to trust. What difference does it make if I'm here or at home? At least here, nobody can get in from the outside. Not unless I let them."

"You don't know that," my father argues.

"I'm not leaving. This is my home now. Where Javi lived. That's where I will live too."

He still wants to argue. But he doesn't. And I know my father well enough to know that he will probably have at least a few armed guards surrounding the place when he leaves here tonight.

"Just think about it, Isa," he says. "Think about coming home."

I walk him to the door.

"The funeral is on Friday," I tell him. "If you want to come."

Chapter 40

Isabella

I thought that maybe this would help. Maybe it would give me some closure to bury Javi. To lay my torment to rest. But the only thing I have learned from this gloomy day is that nothing can lay those feelings to rest.

He is so alone in this cemetery. And I worry that I am doing the wrong thing. Perhaps he should have remained at Moldavia instead.

Only my father has come. Not even River made an appearance. This place feels so cold. So desolate.

At the last minute, I lunge forward, desperate to stop them from laying dirt over him. Over my heart. My father halts me.

"You are doing the right thing, Isa."

It doesn't feel that way. It feels like he is dying all over again. But I don't move. I don't fight. I remain paralyzed. Long after they have finished. Long after night has settled over the earth and into my bones.

"Let me take you home," my father says.

He means his home. But that isn't home to me anymore.

"Take me to Moldavia," I tell him.

He doesn't like it. But he does it anyway.

* * *

Autumn creeps in slowly, and then all at once. It seems that overnight, everything has gone crisp.

I have a routine now. The same routine every day. I work on the nursery. I write my music. I record. And I visit the cemetery.

Each day, I lay a red rose on Javi's stone. And each day my belly grows. With it, my strength does too.

I can feel him.

I can feel him with me. In the air around me. In the scent of the wild roses that now bloom in the conservatory again. Moldavia is full of his energy. But oddly enough, this place isn't. And yet I come here every day. I read him my lyrics. And today is the last song that I have to read him.

When I close the pages of the journal, I know that it is time. I am ready. I drive into the city. Straight to Luke's office. I know he's here because the stench of his alcohol hits me before I even step foot inside. I knock twice, and he answers, more haggard than I've ever seen him.

"You," he growls. "What do you want?"

"I'm ready to come back," I tell him.

He laughs. Shakes his head. And tries to shut the door in my face. I use my foot to intercept him.

"Your contract has been paid off." He makes a wild gesture with his hands. "It's over. You're finished."

"Paid off?"

He looks at me like I'm an idiot, and then his eyes wander to my belly.

"Yes, paid off. By your psychotic boyfriend. You're out. Done. I don't want anything else to do with you."

"Javi?" I whisper.

"Yes, Javi." He scowls and rubs his shoulder as though he's recalling a painful memory.

"He paid you off?"

"Yes." He blinks. "Are you hard of hearing, Isabella? I fucking said that already."

"That's why you didn't come looking for me."

He makes another gesture with his hand. "I'm done with you."

And it's obvious he really is. Whatever happened between him and Javi has left a sour taste in his mouth. There isn't an ounce of desire in his eyes when he looks at me now. But that only strengthens my resolve. I didn't want to play that card with Luke. I didn't want him to think that things would ever be the same between us. That we could go back to the way things were with me as his willing puppet and him pulling the strings.

There is one other thing that Luke loves though. One other thing I know I can use to my advantage. So before he slams the door in my face a second time, I stop him with one simple question.

"What if I said I could make you a lot of money?"

He narrows his eyes at me. Laughs and shakes his head.

"And how exactly do you think you're going to do that, princess?"

"One final show," I propose. "You can have it all. The rights to the music. Just give me ten percent of the profits."

He laughs again.

"Oh, Isabella. You poor, naïve little country bumpkin. Don't you realize that the world has moved on? There were twenty pop princesses ready to take your place the day you walked out."

He's lying, and I know he's lying. Because I can see the fire in his eyes. He's already thinking about how he can spin this.

"Everyone loves a comeback," I tell him.

"Do they?" he smirks. "I don't know if you could call it a comeback when you never really got started in the first place."

I don't take part in his verbal jousting. This is just the way Luke is. And I know how to push his buttons, just as well as he knows how to push mine. He's all about the dramatic effects.

I pull my foot from the door and meet his eyes.

"Fine. I'll go somewhere else, then. I'm sure there are plenty of others who would be interested in what I'm offering."

I turn to leave, and he grabs me by the arm.

"What exactly are you offering?"

He hates himself right now. Serves him right for putting me through hell.

He doesn't want to need me. But I know as well as he does that his career is in the tank after canceling my tour and then losing Megan to another label.

"One show," I tell him. "My way. No fireworks. No smoke. No backup dancers. Nothing but my music, my way."

"So you want a day at the nursing home then?" he scoffs.

I try to yank my arm away, and he stops me again.

"Fine, fine," he grumbles. "I'm listening."

"My piano," I tell him. "I'm going to play on the piano. And

I'm going to sing. That's it. My songs. My choice. My control."

"Then what do you even need me for?"

"You get to publicize it. I know how much you love that media attention. I'm sure that hasn't changed."

"Why would you do this?" he asks. "Why even bother?"

"Because, Luke. I know this may be a difficult concept for you to understand, but once upon a time, I loved music. I loved to sing. And then everything got messed up. I just want closure. One last show. A show where I can put it all out there. Then I can be done. I can move forward. For good."

He mumbles under his breath again before releasing me.

"I'll see what I can do."

And in Luke speak that's a yes. I smile and pat him on the arm. He winces.

"Your boyfriend won't be coming around for this," he says.

My eyes burn as I swallow and avoid his gaze.

"Don't worry. He won't be."

Chapter 41

Javier

    Cold metal taps the base of my skull, stirring me from my delirious slumber.
    It is familiar, this feeling. The heaviness in my body. The barrel of a gun rapping against my head. But it is the smell of earth that I remember most.
    The urge to wretch is strong, and I am still hungover from whatever it is I ingested. When my eyes finally open, everything is blurred.
    The room is dark and small. Cold. Underground. I'm trying to piece it all together. Trying to make sense of it.
    I see Bella's face in my mind. Her screams. Her fear. A surge of adrenaline has me attempting to launch myself upright, but I am swiftly rejected by the confines of my restraints.
    "Easy there, tiger."
    The voice is muffled, but familiar. The build of the man is too when he comes into view. And then I remember.
    Bella's father. His house. The whiskey. This man is the one. The one who took me from my Bella. I try to lunge at him. To kill him. But my movements are still sluggish. My body is still weak. And I am still chained.
    "There's no need for dramatics."
    It's his shoes that I notice first. The same shoes I have seen a hundred times before. Shoes that have graced my own home. Shoes that belong to the man I trusted with my life.

With Bella's life.

When he sees the stark conclusion on my face, he removes the mask and retrieves an apple from his pocket.

"Sorry old pal," River says. "Just the way these things go sometimes, isn't it?"

I look up at him. My oldest friend. My only friend. I thought I had known betrayal before. I thought that nothing could be worse than what Ray Rossi did to me.

But I was wrong.

I still can't accept it. I want to be logical.

River has taken issue with Isabella. He thinks me weak. Perhaps this is his way of trying to make me remember. To continue down the course of revenge that he helped me plan so meticulously.

This is what I tell myself.

"Release me," I demand.

He looks at me, apologetic, but does not move to help me.

"I think you already know, Javi, that I can't do that."

His words cement the doubts in my mind. Years of memories, skewed as I try to make sense of them. I don't know when it happened. I don't know how. River gives me time to process. He has always been good about that. He knows me so well.

"How long?" I ask.

He paces around the room. Looks at me twice while he chews his apple. And then paces some more.

"Since the sanitarium."

The sanitarium.

He was only ten then. It doesn't seem possible. But I know better. I know with the agency, anything is possible. But still, I reason that there must be another explanation. River could never betray me. It never even crossed my mind.

Except for once… when I quickly dismissed it.

Now I know better.

"Luke," I say. "It was you. You were the one who told him I was coming that day. You were the only one who knew."

He looks away again.

"It wasn't me," he mumbles. "But I know who did. And the leak did come from me."

Fucker.

Lying, filthy, scum.

It is the only thing I can think, and River knows it. He won't even meet my eyes.

"You were never unstable," I accuse.

He stops. And now he looks offended.

"I'm as unstable as they come," he assures me. "The back story was true. I wouldn't lie about that, Javi."

"No?" I question. "So only everything else then?"

"I know it might seem that way," he says. "But you should know better than anyone that things are not always how they appear."

"So then tell me how they really are," I demand. "Tell me the truth for once. If you can even bring yourself to do that much."

River appears hurt by my words. His eyes flash before he turns away again.

"I need you to do something for me," he says. "And it isn't sanctioned by the agency."

This much, I believe. If the agency were involved in this, it would not be only River and me in this room. He is desperate. And I have never seen River desperate.

"There is a girl," he begins.

"A girl," I scoff. "You are lying."

This has to be the agency's doing. There must be more to this than what I can see.

River turns to me. Discards the apple core onto the ground. His eyes narrow and sharp.

"It's the truth."

"The truth is that you are a coward and a liar."

River is unfazed by my accusations now, and determination has strengthened his resolve as he continues.

"The program. I was a part of it too."

And now he has my attention. I look up at him. I still don't want to believe him. He is a traitor. A liar. He is no friend of mine.

But then he recites his thirteen-digit code number. The same numbers we all had. The numbers we were assigned upon entrance into the program.

It can't be true.

"I would have known," I tell him. "You were the same age."

"Yes, but I was in a different sector. And they started me earlier."

"How early?" I press.

"Nine."

I shake my head.

River ignores my doubt and goes on to explain.

"I graduated from the program with top marks. Killed three men before the age of ten. I was quite proud of myself."

"Until they sent you to the asylum because you had imagined it all."

He ignores my jab and continues on to his point.

"My first assignment was easy," he says. "Just a man. I do not even remember his face, to be honest. They all blend together after a while. Even the second and the third. I didn't care to know them, or what they had done to earn their deaths. I believed what the agency told me. I followed my orders. I earned my stripes."

He paces again. Looks at me again.

"But then there was the girl."

And now it is me who has tired of his dramatics.

"What girl?"

"She was just a girl," he makes a point to say, as though he hasn't told me three times already.

"There was nothing special about her, really. She was nice to look at as most girls are. She had a pretty face. I thought she would look very pretty when she was dead, and I told her I wouldn't ruin her face because I intended to take her heart."

I think of my Bella. My beautiful Bella. So many times, I had imagined her dead myself. I had imagined how good I thought it would feel to see her that way. Until I tasted her. And she poisoned me. I could not have it any other way.

Before River even admits it, I can tell that he has been poisoned too.

"Those were my instructions," he says. "Cut out her heart. It should have been quite easy. None of the others were difficult."

He struggles with acknowledging his defeat. River has always been too proud. Too arrogant.

"There was something about her face though," he declares. "I thought she was lovely alive. It seemed a shame to watch the life drain from such a pretty face."

He downplays the words, but he cannot hide his true emotion. Not this time. It is clear that River disobeyed his orders long before he ever knew me.

He was a traitor before I ever trusted him. And not only to me.

"You let her live?" I question.

"I let her live," he confesses. "I thought I could fool them. I have always been smarter than most of them."

That much, he does believe.

"It worked, for a while," he says. "I kept her hidden for four years. And I got careless. I thought I could not be touched. That I could do no wrong. They believed I was doing so well. I had made progress with you after all."

I glare at him again. Recalling those initial conversations we used to have. And it is abundantly clear to me now why they paired me with River.

He was sly. He was cunning. And he was so easily able to convince me he was nothing more than a boy. Just like me. A boy who I related to. One who I trusted.

"Before you get angry," River interrupts my thoughts, "Just know this, Javi. My friendship with you was real and sincere. That was not a lie."

"Everything you have told me is a lie," I sneer.

"Not that," he insists. "You were the only friend I had. They made me kill all my others."

I do not feel bad for him. Even when he goes on. Because it doesn't matter. Nothing he says matters anymore. I do not care about this girl or his plight. I only care about his reasons for bringing me here. For keeping me here.

"This story is boring me," I tell him. "If you have a point, River, get to it."

He nods. Retrieves another apple from his pocket and tosses it between his hands.

"They were watching me," he says. "Surreal, I know. It's the agency. But you get comfortable. You get it in your head that you are not the one they don't trust. That you are one of them. You do everything they ask of you. Why would they need to watch you?"

"So they found the girl," I say.

"They found the girl."

He turns away so that I cannot see the emotion on his face. Emotion that is rare for River. I thought he was a sociopath, and I did not judge him for it.

All those times he told me I was weak with Bella, I thought he was right. But I judge him for this because he is the one who is weak now. I tell him as much, but he ignores me.

"When they discovered her, they decided to make an example of me," he says. "They put her into the program. The assassins program."

They turned her into a killer.

Before he even tells me, I know how this story will end. The agency is predictable, at least in this one respect.

"She will come for you," I say.

"She will," he agrees. "And she will try to kill me. They've turned her against me."

"Then she was weak too," I observe.

This time, it is River who sneers in my direction.

"As weak as your Isabella?"

"My Bella has more strength in her little finger than you will ever possess."

"You should hope so," he tells me. "Since you have abandoned her."

His words enrage me. I fight against the chains again, but it is no use. River is a skilled assassin. He would not do anything halfway. And most especially not with the likes of me.

"I did what was best for her," I snarl. "I was wrong. I was wrong to listen to you. To use her for my revenge. She does not deserve to be tortured anymore. She deserves to live in peace."

River stops. His face is serious now. So serious I know that he is not fucking with me this time.

"How can she ever live in peace when she carries your child?"

My limbs grow heavy, and my heartbeat sluggish. There is an ache in the back of my throat. A chill in my spine.

My child?

Isabella carries my child. I need to get to her. I was wrong. So wrong. She believes I am dead. That I have abandoned her. My Bella.

It is pure agony to imagine her, swollen with my baby. Crying in her bed with nothing more than her vile father to comfort her.

"I must go to her," I tell River. "Let me go."

"Sorry," he says again. "But I was making a point before if you'd let me get back to it. This information will only serve to hasten my purpose for you now. And perhaps make you more willing to help."

I thrash against the chains again until I am bloody, screaming out my loathing for him. He waits until I am calm before he explains.

"I am doing you a favor," he insists. "I know you will see this in time."

"You need not worry about your girl," I tell him. "Because I will kill you myself."

"Think of her father," River says. "Of what he did to you, Javi. Are you really ready to let that go?"

I do not answer him. But I can feel the vein in my throat, throbbing. The desire is still there. The desire to kill Ray. I don't know if I can let it go. River knows this. And he is using my own methods on me, quite effectively.

The agency may train us in the art of psychological warfare, but they cannot make us immune to our own methods.

"You only ever had two options, Javi," he says. "In the worst-case scenario, Isabella would have been poisoned by her father. He would have turned her back against you if he hasn't already."

"No," I argue.

"You are a skilled manipulator," River acknowledges. "I will give you this, Jav. But Ray is even more skilled than you or me. It is how he fooled you before. How do you think his own daughter will respond to his tactics?"

I shake my head and try to deny it. I don't want to accept that it could be true. I don't want to believe it. River knows that everyone I have ever cared for has betrayed me, and he is exploiting that in the same way I exploited Isabella's fears.

"Trauma bonding," River continues, "is a powerful weapon. But the bond must remain for that relationship and dependency to flourish. You know as well as I do that Ray would not allow that to happen."

"No," I say again. "Isabella is not like us. She can forgive. She can..."

"That's the lie we all want to believe," River cuts me off. "Just as my girl's feelings were real too. Until the agency got a hold of her. Until they turned her into a killer. Just as our friendship was real, even as I lied to you, Javi. Even as I betrayed you like all the others before you."

"Bella is not that way," I insist.

But even I am starting to doubt myself. I am uncertain if she hates me now, just as I predicted. It was her hope for survival. She had only convinced herself that she cared for me to survive the circumstances of her situation.

"I don't think I need to remind you of the second scenario," River goes on. "But let's be hypothetical for a moment. Say that your Bella is as strong as you insist she is. Say that despite the odds and well documented psychological evidence to the contrary, her feelings for you endured in your absence. Would those feelings sustain even when you murdered her beloved father?"

I do not answer him because I already know the answer. The answer is no. Bella could not love me if I killed Ray. She could not forgive me for that.

"It is bound to happen," River says. "You know it, Jav. I know it. Let's not lie to ourselves anymore, okay? You would have to kill him. It's the only way."

"No," I argue.

"It's not so bad. You have accomplished what you set out to do. You have destroyed Ray by destroying his daughter. And now he must live with those consequences."

"You will not sway me," I tell him. "There is nothing you can say that will stop me from killing you and going back to Bella."

River sighs. Then he stops tossing the apple between his palms to meet my gaze.

"Nothing?" he repeats. "Oh but Jav, I'm afraid you're wrong about that."

Chapter 42

Javier

The scent of tobacco is the first thing to hit me. Tobacco and pipe smoke.

I see his shoes before I ever see his face. It's always the shoes that I remember. The shoes that have walked in and out of my life over the years. Shoes give away so much about a man. The way he wears them. The way he maintains them.

And in Ray Rossi's case, it is the way he shines them so meticulously. Cleaning up the evidence of where he's been. The things he has done.

My mother always told me that if someone's shoes were too clean, it was because they had something to hide. In that respect, I believe she was right.

Ray has many secrets and many faces.

He hides his true nature well. Especially now, in his older years. Beneath the fuzzy gray of his mustache and the softness in his fading eyes, there lurks a master of exploitation.

I was only a boy when he came for me. A boy who had lost everything. A boy who the world believed had viciously killed his own mother. And Ray was the only one who looked at me as if I did not.

He disguised himself. A wolf in sheep's clothing. I wanted to believe he would help me. But once upon a time, I wanted to believe that my mother would get better too.

Now here we are, years later. I am a man, and he is old and gray. I intended to exact my revenge. I planned it out so precisely. But instead, I fell in love with his daughter.

"Surprised to see me, Javier?" he asks.

I do not reply but instead look to River. He remains by the door, silent. The friend I trusted, working with my enemy all along.

"You should not be," Ray says. "You must have known this day would come. You must have known the moment you touched Isa, you would die."

This time, I do meet his eyes. And I make it known that I am no longer a boy. His threats mean nothing to me, and Ray must know there is nothing he can do that is worse than what I put his daughter through.

I was a monster to her. And still, she fell in love with me. I smile, thinking of her beautiful face.

"It was worth it," I tell him.

He clocks me with the pair of brass knuckles he reserves for such occasions. Ray is weak in his older years. He relies on weapons because his muscles fail him.

Blood leaks from my mouth and I spit it onto the dirty floor. I can't help myself. I can't help but long for his suffering.

"She still wants for me," I say to him. "She will always want for me. I am inside of her. In her mind. In her heart. She will never be free of me, even in death. Your beloved daughter fell for the monster you created, Ray. How does that make you feel?"

He hits me again. Three times. Until it becomes too much for him. Until a coughing fit seizes him and spittle flies from his mouth.

"I will rid her of your poison, even if I have to cut it out myself."

The world around me falls silent, and River turns his gaze to the floor. My vision clouds and adrenaline floods every fiber of my muscles, straining against the chains that bind me.

I will slaughter him with my bare hands. I will drain the remaining light from his eyes, and I will not regret it. Not anymore.

"That's right," Ray taunts. "I will be the one to take that child and destroy it the moment it is born. Now tell me how that feels."

I struggle against the chains until I no longer can. Until I am out of breath myself. Until I am bloody and spent and completely at his mercy. Ray merely laughs at me.

River remains motionless by the door. And I cannot believe I have been so blind. I allowed my own love for Bella to influence this grand illusion. I mistakenly believed that as sick as Ray was, he still loved his own daughter.

Now I know that I was wrong.

I should have killed him when I had the chance. The moment I learned he was back, I should have shot him where he lay. And now, I must pay the consequences for my weakness. I told my Bella that I would protect her. I have failed her all over again.

"We should move now," River says. "There will be plenty of time to toy with him later."

Ray swivels his head around and scowls in his direction.

"It's time when I say it's time."

River is a traitor, of this I am certain. But it seems that we have a common enemy. I don't know how I could have missed it. I don't know how I didn't see it before. All those times he encouraged me. How he helped me plan out the systematic destruction of Ray through Isabella. The way he whispered in my ear and never let me forget my revenge. The way he told me over and over that Isabella could never care for me. That I must remember the plan.

It was in his mind all along.

And instead of Isabella, it was I who was the pawn in this game.

A knock sounds at the door and River looks to Ray for approval. Ray nods, and River opens it.

The heat is stifling. Sand blows in from above, indicating that we are in the desert somewhere.

"We have to move now, sir," the voice on the other side says.

Ray nods again and gestures the men inside. They surround me, and Ray makes a point to show me that they are all well-armed.

"Make one move, and die now," he tells me.

They haul me up from the floor and unchain me. Six of them drag me out into the blistering sun and shove me into the back of a suburban.

"Ten minutes," someone says.

And then, we leave.

Chapter 43

Javier

They take me into the middle of the desert. If it weren't for the compound in the distance, I would assume this to be my final resting place.

Instead, they free my hands and shove me out of the truck. I don't need to ask where we are. I know this area well. This is the same compound where I lived for the remainder of my childhood. The one where Ray took me when I left the asylum.

Here, I was trained in computers. Math. Killing.

Ray searches my face for any sign of emotion. But there is none. I can only think of my Bella now. Of the child that she carries inside of her. I will do anything to protect them. I will do anything to get them back. And for now, that means playing by Ray's rules.

He recites a thirteen-digit number and tells me to repeat it back to him.

River's eyes shift around anxiously, and I know this is for him. This is what he gets for betraying me and fulfilling his end of the bargain.

"Delete everything on file," Ray tells me. "Bring the girl to me when you are finished. And perhaps I can find it in my heart to be merciful. Perhaps the child my daughter births will be adopted into a nice family rather than a dumpster."

My fists curl at my sides, and the guards raise their weapons.

"I am giving you one last opportunity here, Javi," Ray says. "Do not underestimate my reach. There are many others who would gladly take this task and complete it much faster than you. And they have much less to lose."

I remain silent. Steadfast in my resolve. I am doing this for Bella. Even knowing that when I come back, there will likely be a bullet in my skull.

I can't trust Ray. But I know Ray. I don't doubt his words. He will destroy the child that he knows is mine. He will do it while he tells himself it is what is best for Isabella. I must find another way to end this.

I turn to head for the compound, but Ray's voice stops me.

"Enjoy your trip down memory lane."

I curb the urge to kill him all over again by thinking of my Bella. I think of what I need to do, and I focus on that alone.

And I walk. Silently through the desert. Leaving Ray and River behind. There is a reason they chose me for this task. Despite what Ray says, this task could not be completed by anyone.

I am the only operative who ever managed to disable the entire compound security system. Not once, but twice. Today will make number three.

It has been many years since I have been at this particular compound, but much is still the same. Including the guards who watch over the control room. They are older now, but I remember them just fine. Fear reflects briefly in their eyes when they see me for the first time.

I kill them with their own weapons, and I take satisfaction in knowing that they no longer breathe the air of this scorched earth.

The security system has updated with the times too. It is much more sophisticated than when I was here. But like the system, I am adaptable.

It is not easy to navigate. It has already been thirty minutes. With each passing minute, I am more likely to get caught. It's taking me too long. And Ray's patience is not infinite.

Just as I find my way into the system, a shadow passes over the door frame. Another guard. He draws his weapon, and I fire first.

The body count is growing, and this is messier than I would have preferred. But with a few more clicks of the keyboard, I am finally in.

I find the file for the operative that Ray gave me, glancing briefly at her photo to identify her and her location, and then I delete.

I delete everything.

The process takes another five minutes. When it is complete, I hesitate before leaving. Ray would expect me to leave the system as it was. He wanted this done quietly.

I smile. Because I always did like irony. I unlock the cell doors. All but hers. And then I shut down the power to the entire building. It is up to them now to escape. To overpower the guards and take what is rightfully theirs.

Freedom.

I leave the control room and walk down the hall that I know by heart. It is the same hall where I was kept for so many years. I open her cell door manually and shine my flashlight inside. She is sitting on her bed. Small and fragile in appearance.

"Come," I tell her. "We are leaving this place."

She glances up at me and shakes her head.

"I don't want to leave."

Her voice is soft.

It's obvious she has been broken, just as River said. It is also obvious why he cares for her. She does have a pretty face as he said. But there is nothing particularly special about her that I can see. She is not like my Bella. Then again, nobody really is.

"I don't have time," I say. "And I'd prefer not to hurt you."

She rises from the bed and walks in my direction. I think that this is good. She is going to comply, and we can leave. Only this isn't what happens. Because the girl punches me in the throat.

She snarls and tries to make her escape around me. I stop her with a hand around her throat. And then she socks me in the gut.

Of all the things I had to do in this compound, fighting a girl was my least favorite.

I release her, and we go hand to hand. Her shots are sharp and precise. I was wrong about her. She is not fragile at all. In body or mind. She lands many painful blows that would disable me had I been younger and less accustomed to the pain. But I am not.

And as well as she has been trained, I have many years of experience over her. I identify her weakness almost immediately and put her in a choke hold.

"I am sorry," I tell her. "But for now you must sleep."
And within a minute, she does.

Chapter 44

Isabella

Everything Luke has ever done has been on a grand scale. The PR for the show is much of the same. Tickets sold out within minutes. It makes me nervous. It makes me content. As content as I can be with a broken heart.

This show is for him.

An entire catalog of our time together.

The songs I wrote from my first moments in captivity to the moments I fell in love with Javi. And then… the songs that express my grief in the only way that I can.

It is a timeline of our entire relationship. A small blip in the enormous number of seconds and hours that have compiled my life. But these seconds and hours I spent with him are the ones that have impacted me most.

The ones that will haunt me for the rest of my days. The ones that I will treasure. There is only one thing I need to complete the story. One more song for the final chapter.

You can't choose who you love, for better or worse.

But there is one thing that will determine the way that I remember Javi. The thing that will help me to understand him. To have my closure. The thing that will provide me with the lyrics for one last song. And this thing cannot be found at Moldavia.

In fact, there is only one place that it can be found.

And I am not certain that anyone else even knows this place exists. Except for me. Because I am paranoid, like my father. And because I did not trust him after Javi was poisoned. I tracked him up here into this cabin in the middle of the woods.

As I stand here in the clearing, I know that this is where my answers lie.

I have observed my father closely over the years. I have witnessed the fashion in which he sought out devices. The places he would hide things he did not want found.

I am well informed of the precautions he takes and the way he goes about his security measures. And this is how I know that what I'm looking for will not be inside the cabin at all. When I find the loose floorboard on the porch, I know I am right.

I lift it up and reveal the visibly undisturbed earth below. A trick my father once taught me. To everyone else, it looks like nothing. Just dirt. To me, it looks like a tarp below, covering something else. Something more sinister.

I am right.

When I brush my hand over the dirt, there is plastic beneath. I pull it up, only to reveal a shoebox below.

It is not high tech. Anything the agency would have my father keep would not be kept here. This is something he has done on his own. In a hurry. Something he intended to come back to. And I must get to it first, whatever it is.

I don't look inside. I take the shoebox and replace the tarp, covering it with dirt. Then I leave, checking my mirrors the entire drive back to Moldavia.

My heart is racing, and my palms are sweating, and I am afraid of the answers this box might carry. Something that once opened cannot be undone. But I have come to realize that what Javi said rings true.

Nobody can hurt me anymore. I have a built a fortress around my heart. Whatever this box contains, I can handle it. No matter how sinister. I am ready to know the truth.

I am ready to learn my father's secrets.

So, when I am secure inside of Moldavia, I open it up. On top, there is a file. An old file, with handwritten notes. It takes me some time to read the messy scrawl. But it is clear from the header that it is a medical record. For Javi's mother. It speaks of her illness. Her mental decline. The tumor in her brain. An incurable tumor.

Her illness was not random. It was because of the tumor. A tumor that would prove fatal in time, as evidenced by these very notes. What I can't understand is why my father would keep the file hidden away like this. Why it would matter to him.

There is so much paperwork that most of it seems irrelevant. It is the entire history of her medical records from the time she was first diagnosed to her last appointment.

And then there are transcripts. At first, I think they are part of her records as well. Until I see the dates. They were after her death.

They are transcripts from something else. An interview performed by my father. An interview of Javi. He was only a child at the time. Eleven years old. It was after his mother had died.

I read through the entire transcript. Three times. My father always told me how dangerous Javi was. He told me how he had killed his mother, and what a tragedy it was. But it was never true.

The truth is right here, printed in ink. A truth that I can no longer deny. My father has been lying to me for so long. But even worse, he has been lying to Javi. Javi told him what happened that day. He told him how his mother believed there was a device implanted in her stomach. That she had to retrieve it. How she made Javi watch as she gutted herself like a fish and tried to perform her own surgery. She died of the blood loss, despite Javi's best efforts to save her.

It is a secret he has lived with his whole life. Allowing everyone around him to believe he was a murderer. That he murdered his own mother in cold blood. And my father has not only condoned the lie, but he has perpetuated it.

He turned Javi into a killer on the basis that he already was one. He inserted him into the operative training program and left him there.

A child.

He was only a child.

And I was wrong before that nothing could hurt me.

Whatever was left of my heart has now disintegrated. It aches in a way that there is no cure for. This is a memory that will haunt me for eternity.

I don't know how my father can look himself in the mirror every day. But I can't stop. There is a hunger inside of me to know more. To know everything. So I keep digging. And in the bottom of the box, I find six more tapes. Numbered, just as the ones hidden away in Javi's wall were.

They are identical to those tapes. In brand and size. It is not a coincidence. It didn't make sense for Javi to keep those tapes hidden away if they were blank. And it wouldn't make sense for my father to have the same amount of tapes, with the same numbers.

The only conclusion that I can draw is that my father replaced them with blanks and took the real tapes.

I head to the conservatory and fire up the projector. I start in order, with the first tape. The image flickers to life, and it is Javi. Javi as a child. A child in the operative program. Being tortured. Burned. Beaten. Interrogated. Trained.

I can't look away from the horrors on the screen. Not this time. I owe him this much. No matter how dreadful it is, I owe it to him to feel his pain. To understand it. Even if it is too late.

My father comes to visit him in the tapes. He sits across from him at a steel table and asks Javi to give him progress reports. Javi refuses to speak to him. Sometimes he is strong. Stubborn. But there are times when he cries. When he pleads with my father to take him home with him as he promised.

My father always says the same thing. Soon. Another lie. One so easily spoken from his lips. It is something I can't comprehend. I feel as though I am losing my mind. I feel as though I am watching a movie that isn't real.

I don't know how this man can be so different from the one who raised me. The only father that I knew. The one who was distant and busy, but always loving. Fiercely protective. They were two different men.

One good.

One evil.

But they both lived in my father's body. They both inhabited his mind. And they are both responsible for the horrors that were done to Javi. Horrors that I can no longer refute. I have seen the evidence. I have seen all that I need to know.

I watch the tapes on repeat. Until I am consumed with hatred and sadness. With rage and regret. Until there is nothing left for me to do but to put pen to paper and write one more song.

My last song.

Chapter 45

Javier

I toss the girl over my shoulder and drag her through the desert. Within minutes, the compound is in chaos behind us.

This desert landscape is unforgiving, but it is no match for those with a thirst for freedom. And these operatives do thirst for freedom.

Their figures scatter around me in the distance. I pay them no mind, and they do not bother me either. My only focus is on the horizon, up behind the dune where I know River and Ray will be.

I do not have many bartering chips. At this point, I only have one. Ray is not invested in her life, but I know River will do anything for her. It does not give me much to work with, but she is the only hope I have.

When I reach the top of the dune, I have my freshly acquired weapon at the ready, targeted directly to the back of her skull. But River knows me well.

He has prepared for the occasion. The guards have either been dismissed or disposed of elsewhere, and only Ray lies bloody and helpless at his feet.

River has his own gun trained on Ray's face, but his eyes are on me.

"Let the girl go, Javi," he instructs.

"Why should I?" I challenge. "It makes no difference to me whether Ray lives or dies."

"Oh?" he arches a brow. "And what of your Bella? What would you tell her about daddy dearest? How he died like a dog in the desert after he had finally come home. And would she believe you?"

He knows very well that she wouldn't. How could she after all that I have done to her? After the lengths I have gone to for my revenge. Bella would not believe that I did not kill her father. And I don't know that she could ever forgive me for such an offense either.

"You know she wouldn't," River answers my unspoken thought. "How could she?"

"I will trade you then," I tell him. "The girl for Ray. The deal is done. You have no reason to kill him."

River considers my proposition. Despite his cool demeanor, he is desperate. River does not really know how to handle desperate. His eyes keep darting to the girl, trying to get a look at her face. But he cannot.

Not like this.

She is starting to rouse, and everything is going to go to shit if he does not make a decision soon. She makes a noise in the back of her throat, and River straightens his posture.

"Fine," he says. "Fine. On the count of three, old friend."

River counts.

I have always been a man of my word. But he has not. On three, he steps away from Ray. I release the girl and step back. She wakes- bound and startled- and her eyes move straight to River. Recognition flashes followed up with rage.

She struggles against her restraints in an attempt to get to him, and River breathes her name, low and quiet.

It is a secret to him. One that he does not wish to share with the world.

"It has been so long," he says. "I know you are angry. Confused. But in time, this will change."

"In time, I will cut your throat," she snarls.

He looks away from her, unable to bear witness to her wrath. His eyes seek out mine, full of remorse.

"Old friend, I have always cared for you. That was never a lie. You must know this."

"I can no longer believe anything you say to be true," I answer.

He nods in understanding. And then he looks at the girl again.

"For you, my love."

He shoots Ray in the head. Without warning. Without hesitation. I have already raised my gun, but it is too late.

His is aimed straight for my face.

Chapter 46

Isabella

I am making a cup of tea when the doorbell rings.

The doorbell never rings. Not here at Moldavia. I retrieve the small pistol that I took from my father's house and move towards the door.

"Isabella," a voice speaks from the other side. "It's me."

My chest expands with air, and in a moment, I forget that I can no longer trust him. He is not a friend. But it doesn't matter.

The only thing my mind can comprehend right now is that he is back.

He is the last link to Javi that I have. I keep the gun in my hand and open the door. River stands on the other side, apple in hand. Relaxed as ever. Casual as ever. But there is something very different about him.

His usual smirk is absent, and instead, his eyes are heavy and flat.

"Are you going to invite me in for a cup of tea?" he asks.

"No," I answer. "But you can come in for the truth if you'd like."

He gives me a stiff nod and joins me inside. The pistol remains clutched in my hand as he takes a seat at the counter island. I maintain a safe distance from the other side.

He eyes the weapon but does not appear to be bothered by it. I don't expect him to. Some men hide their evil well. Men like my father. Men like River.

"You betrayed him," I whisper.

I can't keep the tears from falling this time. I can't help getting emotional as I recall the horrifying details of Javi's childhood.

"How could you?" I snap. "He thought you were his friend."

River has the decency to look ashamed, and his voice reflects his guilt when he responds.

"I know," he answers. "It is why I am here now. To make amends."

"There are no amends," I say. "It's done. It's over. The chance for that has passed. There will never be another one again."

River does not argue me on this point, but instead goes on to say what he came to.

"I have always loved Javi like a brother. I did not do right by him, and for that I am sorry. It is something I will have to live with. But I had my reasons. And I think he would understand, had he been in the same position."

"You just left," I say. "You didn't come to his funeral. There was a funeral. Did you even know that? I had to bury him, alone. Without anyone in the world who loved him. It's not fair, River. You should have been there."

"Isabella, I know you are upset. But the reason I have come to you today is not because of Javi."

I blink and try to make sense of the gravity in his voice. I don't know what it could be. What could be so serious that isn't about Javi?

"It's your father," he tells me. "Isabella…"

His voice is broken, soft. And only slightly apologetic now.

"I don't know how to tell you this. But your father is dead. And I am the one who killed him."

Chapter 47

Javier

My Bella is beautiful under the spotlight.

The room is dim. Intimate. The seats are sold out. And it is not like most concerts. There is no screaming. There is no talking. There is complete silence when she takes her place on the bench, and they all hold their breath. Waiting for my angel to sing.

She adjusts the microphone and glances nervously into the crowd before turning away again. She speaks softly at first. Holding a hand over her belly. The place where my child grows inside of her.

"This is a new song," she says. "It's called Words Only You Can Hear."

She looks towards the ceiling and closes her eyes, a solitary tear rolling down her cheek as her fingers begin to roam over the keys.

The music is soft and beautiful, just like Bella. And the words are songs she sang only for me. At Moldavia.

It is the first of many songs. She has been busy in my absence. Busy writing and playing. This show is a time capsule of our journey together, and then hers alone. She sings of her pain those first few months. Her fear.

And then later, her love.

She sings of her anguish when I left her. Of her anger. And then, of her solitude.

The last and final song, she dedicates to her father. But it is not what I expect. It is anguish again. Anguish over his lies, and her questioning who he really was. Torment over the things he did. And I know by the time the music has finished playing that she has learned the truth.

She knows he is dead.

And she knows the parts of me I could never bring myself to tell her about. I don't know how. But my Bella is smart. She is curious. And in my absence, she has only grown stronger.

The room is still silent. The crowd holds their breath while they wait for her to speak again.

And finally, she rises from the bench. Like a phoenix rising from the flames. Her head held high. Her grief behind her.

She picks up the microphone one last time before the crowd erupts into applause.

"Thank you."

Chapter 48

Isabella

Security ushers me back to the dressing room where Luke greets me at the door.

"Out of the fucking park," he says. "Baby, you were out of the fucking park."

"Thank you, Luke."

"So..."

He lingers in place, blocking my entry.

"So?"

"Let's talk next show. World tour. Isabella, you have to give them more."

He's got dollar signs in his eyes, and I'm already shaking my head.

"I told you the deal, Luke. One show. One time. That's it. I'm done. I'm out of the game for good."

His shoulders fall, and he still doesn't want to accept it.

"Baby doll, c'mon, did you not see that crowd out there? They were wild for you. You have to ride the wave."

"There is no wave," I tell him. "This was it, Luke."

"So that's it?" he repeats. "You're just going to give all this up and go back to your hole and be a mom?"

I smile, despite the horrified expression on his face.

"That's exactly what I'm going to do."

"Unbelievable," he mutters. "Unbelievable. You're going to miss it, Isabella. You're going to want this back. This feeling. But you won't be able to have it. Not if you wait too long."

"It's okay," I assure him. "I'll live with it if I do."

He sighs. Shuffles from side to side.

"Will you call me if you change your mind?"

"You'll be the first number I dial."

He moves in for a creepy hug, and I hold my hand out instead. He shakes it, and then reluctantly moves along. I open the door to my room and sit down. Closing my eyes and taking a deep breath.

That's when it hits me.

The scent. The unmistakable scent of wild roses. I open my eyes to find the stems laid out on my dressing table.

Crimson red.

Tears fill my eyes. I don't dare to hope. I don't dare to fear. But there is knife right beside them. A knife that is all too familiar.

"My sweet Bella."

The voice comes from behind me, so soft I can't be sure I'm not going insane. I can't move. I don't dare. I am so afraid that if I blink, that if move even a fraction of an inch, the illusion in the reflection will disappear. His face will disappear, and I will be plunged right back into my waking nightmare again.

"You have two choices," he tells me. "You can keep me, or you can kill me. For I cannot go on living without you. And I cannot go on living with you as my captive. So you must decide on your own. You must choose to be my willing captive. You must choose to remain by my side for the days of your life, or be merciful and have your vengeance by bleeding me dry."

A tear falls down my cheek, followed by another. And then another. Soon, Javi is kneeling before me at my feet, cupping my face in his palms. And they feel so real. So warm.

I can smell him. I can feel him. It is either the cruelest fabrication of my mind or the best day of my life.

Javi wipes away my tears.

"Do not cry for me, my Bella."

"You can't be real," I whisper. "This can't be real. I must be dreaming."

"It is no dream," he assures me.

I close my eyes and open them again. He is still there. Still breathing. His heart still beating when I feel it beneath my palm.

"Javi?"

"Yes, my love," he answers. "It is me. I am real. I am here. And I am not going anywhere."

I leap into his arms, and he catches me.

"Javi."

Over and over, I say his name like a prayer. He kisses me. He holds me. And he doesn't let go. His eyes move over my body. Over the bump that now rests between us.

"You carry my child so well, my Bella."

His hand hovers there nervously, wishing to touch, but possibly afraid.

"You can," I tell him. "This baby is ours, Javi."

He touches me, as gently as Javi has ever touched me.

"I still cannot believe it is real," he says.

"Did you know?" I ask.

There are so many questions. So much for us to talk about. I don't know where he was or what happened to him. But I don't know if I'm even ready to hear it yet, and I think Javi knows it.

"I did know, Bella," he answers. "There is much for us to discuss."

"There is," I agree. "One step at a time. I only just got you back."

"I take it then," he says hopefully, "you do not wish to kill me?"

"Don't ever leave me again," I tell him. "Ever."

"I won't, my Bella," he says. "But your father…"

I shake my head and close my eyes.

"No. Not now."

Maybe not ever.

I don't know how to make sense of the things that I feel for my father. My warring grief and hatred for the man that he was. I think I will always be split in two as far as he is concerned.

I mourn him because I am still his daughter. But I have so much anger towards him too. Anger that I never had a chance to express. But none of that matters right now.

Nothing else matters when Javi is real, and he is right here beside me.

I tell him as much.

And then I tell him to take me home.

Chapter 49

Isabella

"My Bella."

Javi's voice pulls me from my daydream, and I open my eyes. The sun is shining, but his body shields my face from the worst of it.

The hammock rocks in the breeze and I cradle my belly, resting the book I was reading atop the bump as I give him my full attention.

"What is it?"

"You have been out here too long," he says. "Your skin will burn in this light."

Concern mars his features, and I give him a gentle smile. He is unguarded. Still wild, as he always has been. But there is something so different about my Javi now.

He is no longer ashamed of his scars. He no longer hides from me. He is beautiful and primitive. He still struggles with control. With asking questions or making suggestions instead of demanding them.

Like right now when I can see he would prefer to simply pick me up and carry me back into the house. But he is trying to be patient.

He is trying to learn. We are trying to learn together. I teach Javi patience, and he teaches me strength, and together we make it from one day to the next.

"Bella," he says again. "Come inside, yes?"

"Yes," I answer him. "I will."

"Now?"

He is anxious. The baby will be here any day.

"I need help."

I hold out my hands, and Javi tugs me up from the hammock, cradling me in his arm as he walks me into the house. We sit down at the kitchen island, and he makes me a cup of tea while I watch.

Since his return home, Javi has been busy remodeling Moldavia. The first thing to go was the surgery room. The walls of the house have been re-papered and painted, and the floors polished and shined. The only thing that remains is the locks on the windows. I feel more secure knowing they are in place.

Javi no longer works for the agency. He tells me that they will not come for us, but I can never really feel one hundred percent comfortable when it comes to the agency.

I don't know if I'll ever feel completely comfortable again. If I'll ever stop looking over my shoulder or checking the house for devices.

I know Javi won't either. I see him doing the same. And now that we are about to be parents, it weighs heavy on both of our minds.

That is not the only thing weighing heavy on Javi's mind, and it is obvious in the way he carries himself today.

When he places my tea on the counter, I reach for his hand.

"Javi."

"Hmm, my love?"

He seems scattered, his thoughts elsewhere.

"It's going to be okay."

"What is?" he asks.

"You're going to do just fine."

I tell him so every day, but he doesn't believe me. I know he worries that he will not be a good father. He never had a father, he said. Or at least, he did not know him. And the closest he had to one was my father. The man who deceived him.

"You will be nothing like him," I say. "You will be here. You will be present. And you will teach your son to be a man of honor."

"Yes," he says softly. "I hope so."

I smile and take a sip of my tea.

And then my water breaks.

Javi is still at war in his own mind, and I have to call his name to get his attention.

"Yes, my love?"
"I guess there's no time like the present to find out."
"What do you mean?"
"It's time," I tell him.

Chapter 50

Javier

The whole process is overwhelming from the start.

The trip to the hospital takes an eternity, and I worry I will not get her there on time. The registration process overwhelms me. Paperwork this, and insurance that.

These are things not to worry about I try to tell them. We can take care of it later. But first, we must have our baby. They tell me this is not the way this works, and I get frustrated.

Bella reaches for my hand and smiles.

I know I must be patient. I must do this right, for her. I fill out the paperwork as they ask. Nurses come and go from the room. A doctor comes and goes.

I think that the baby will come soon, but they tell me no, this is not how it works. So we wait. And I watch Bella. This is not the kind of pain I like to see her in.

Eventually, they say she is getting close. They give her an epidural, and I almost get sick. I do not like hospitals. I do not like the smell. The needles. The tools.

I remember my mother, and then I try to erase those thoughts from my memory. Not today. Not ever again.

Forward. Always forward with my Bella.

The doctor comes in and tells her it's time to push. She does. They ask me if I want to see the baby's head, and Bella tells me no. That I better not dare to look down there right now. So I don't.

I stay up by her side and hold her hand and kiss her forehead and tell her how amazing I think she is. How lucky I am to have her. How I will never let her go. She cries and tries to smile. She cannot say the words back. But I don't need them. Not anymore. I know that when she does say them, she means them.

I know that I love her. Nothing will ever come between us again. I tell her so. And she agrees.

"Yes, Javi. Never."

The baby is born, and the doctor laughs as he cleans him up.

"Would you like to meet your daughter?"

"Daughter?" we both ask.

"Yes, it appears that your son is not a son after all. What we have here is a little girl."

Bella smiles and I almost pass out.

A girl.

A girl is not better, is it?

A girl is worse?

A girl is sensitive. Delicate.

This means I must learn to be sensitive and delicate. I'm still panicking over this until I look at my Bella. So soft and beautiful and exhausted, clutching our baby girl in her arms.

She looks up at me, and there are tears in her eyes.

"She's so…"

Her voice is weak. Raspy. She must be so tired, I reason.

"Pretty."

The word is barely a breath.

A machine starts beeping. The doctor yells something. But I can only focus on Bella. Her eyes have closed, and her body is limp, and I only blinked, and I don't understand what's happening.

Someone shoves the baby into my arms and tells me I must leave. I tell them no. The machines keep beeping, and Bella is not waking up, and I am so scared. The most afraid I have ever been, with such a tiny baby in my arms.

I cannot fight them. I cannot get to them. Because it would hurt the baby. The nurses push me from the room, and I tell them no again.

"Mr. Castillo," the nurse says. "You must be calm. You have to let us try to help her."

But that isn't the way it sounds. That isn't the way it sounds at all. Because her voice is grim, and her eyes are apologetic. She's looking at me like my Bella is already gone. And the only thing I can do is look down at the little baby in my arms.

The little baby that looks so much like Bella.

Epilogue

Javier

-Four years later-

"Aria, come to Papa."

The little girl with black hair and pale blue eyes bounds from the other end of the room and leaps up onto the sofa.

"What is it, Papa?" she asks.

I tap her on the nose and shake my head. "It is long past your bedtime, yes?"

She giggles and shrugs.

"I'm not tired, though."

"Ah yes, this is what you say. However, in the morning it will be, Papa I'm too tired to get out of bed."

She giggles again.

"Can you tell me one story first?"

Like most things, I cannot turn her down when she uses this voice. The same one she got from her mother.

She is a songbird, like her mother too.

"Which story would you like tonight, my Aria? Will it be Kings and Queens or fairies and toads?"

"I want the story about the caged bird," she tells me.

I smile.

My heart aches whenever I tell this story, but I indulge her. It is good for me, to never forget.

"Come, come." I pat the sofa beside me and Aria cuddles into my side.

"Okay, here we go. You comfortable?"

"Yes, Papa," she says.

"Okay then. Once upon a time, there was a beautiful songbird. The most beautiful songbird in all the land."

"You forgot the most important part," Aria interrupts me.

"I have not forgotten. You just need to learn patience, my Aria. Now hush and let your Papa tell the story."

"Okay," she whispers.

"The beautiful songbird looked just like you. With long raven hair and pale blue eyes. Her skin was porcelain, and she could have been an angel who fell from the sky."

"Soooooo pretty," Aria adds.

"Yes, she was. And this beautiful songbird had the voice of an angel too. But sometimes, she did not always know this to be true. She was filled with doubt by all the villagers who told her she did not sing so well as she thought."

"They were sooooo mean," Aria contributes.

"Yes, they were mean. But the meanest of all was the beast that she crossed paths with one fateful day. He thought her so beautiful that he decided he should have her for himself. But it was not to covet her like the songbird she was. The beast had set out to hurt the songbird."

"But why, Papa?" Aria asks. "Why would he want to do that?"

"I have told you this story many times," I say.

She grins.

"I know, but not for a while now."

"Okay," I concede. "Well the Beast, he was cold-hearted, Aria. Not like you. He did not care for others. He had no compassion. His heart was filled with hate and a thirst for revenge. Because the songbird's father had tricked him once. And because he was scarred and ugly. He decided that it was easier to have his revenge than to accept what was."

"So he did not think the songbird could love him?" Aria asks.

"No," I answer. "He did not. For he was a beast after all."

"But sometimes, maybe, a songbird could love a beast anyway," Aria says thoughtfully. "Right, Papa?"

"Yes." I smile. "You are so smart, Aria. And this is precisely what happened. In spite of his terrible ways, the songbird fell in love with the beast, anyway."

Aria wiggles her feet beside me nervously in anticipation for the part that she remembers next.

"But it was not to be. For there was a terrible, terrible illness that took…"

"Papa!" Aria covers her ears and screeches. "Don't say this part."

I poke her in the tummy, and she smiles.

"But this is the story, Aria. Do you want to hear it or not?"

"I do, but skip to the best part."

"Patience," I mumble. "You must learn patience, my Aria."

"Okay," she yawns. "Then let's finish the story tomorrow night."

She closes her eyes and snuggles against me, and I do not have the heart to move her. Instead, I stroke her hair beneath my palm and marvel over the little girl that Isabella and I created.

"Do we miss mama?" I ask her.

She yawns again and nods into my side, her answer only a faint whisper.

"Yes, Papa. We miss her very much."

And then she is asleep. Off to dreams in a place that no darkness can touch her.

I close my eyes too and remember my Bella. I remember her in a white dress, with her hair falling in curls around her face. She wore a halo of roses that day, and I told her that I thought it was shameful I was the only one to bear witness to such beauty.

She argued with me that the minister was there to witness it too, and all the stars in the sky above us, and of course, our Aria.

I told her I had no need for the stars in the sky or the moon or the sun, because I had her, and that was everything to me. She replied with a smile on her face that I had gone soft, and she was probably right.

But my vows were not soft. And the ceremony was not soft. I was determined to bind her to me for life, and words weren't enough. Her blood still hangs in a vial around my neck, where it will remain until my heart gives out.

My Bella conceded that this was the way it should be because our journey had never been all roses.

I laid claim to her with my ring and my words and my knife. The minister paled as we performed the blood ceremony and exchanged vows.

I promised to love, cherish, and protect my wife. And then I promised to punish and reward her when I saw fit too.

Bella promised to love me, even when I didn't deserve it. She promised to teach me patience when I needed it, which was always. And she promised that even if I lived to earn another thousand scars, she would see nothing except for her beautiful beast.

The last part was not necessary. Because I discovered that as time went on, my scars faded away. Perhaps not in the mirrors, but in my own eyes. It was easy to forget they existed when Bella loved me in spite of them. Her opinion was the only one that mattered. The only one that still matters.

And I miss her terribly sometimes when she disappears this way. When she goes away to write. Vanishing into the other wing of the house for hours on end.

It is something that helps her. It is her way of processing the emotions that she feels so strongly at times. I will often hear the soft notes of the piano at all hours of the night, playing songs with words only I can hear.

She does not put them on albums. She simply records them and uploads them to YouTube. Something for her fans that costs nothing. And then she leaves them, never to return again.

She does not read the comments. She remains safe in her bubble here with her family. Ever since that day when we brought our little girl home.

It took some time to make this happen. I almost lost her. We almost lost her. To an embolism. But against the odds, she recovered.

The doctors told me she was a fighter. And I told them they had no idea. I brought my Bella home, and we have never looked back.

The door opens, and with it comes the light.

"I wasn't expecting you to finish so early."

"I know," Bella says. "But I missed you guys."

She looks lovely this evening, her tired eyes roaming over Aria and then me. She is always so lovely.

"Let me put her to bed," she says. "And then I'll come to you."

I scoop Aria into my arms and hand her to Bella. She leaves, and I go to the place where it all began, amongst the roses and stars.

Bella meets me in the conservatory and pulls me against her, stretching up on her toes to kiss me goodnight. She always kisses me like it's the last time now.

We always treat each day like it may be our last.

Bella has taught me patience, and I have taught her strength, and together we overcome every obstacle life has thrown our way. We have both learned that nothing can break those who have already been broken like us.

"You are still my monster," she tells me.

I kiss her again, just to be sure she knows I mean it.

"And you are still mine. Forever."

Thank you so much for reading BEAST. If you enjoyed it, please consider leaving an honest review on Amazon or Goodreads. You can keep an eye out for my other book releases by signing up for my newsletter at www.azavarelli.com

Acknowledgments

There are so many people that I would like to express my gratitude towards, but it would be impossible to name all of them.

It takes an army to make a book successful, and I am so fortunate to have an abundance of amazing people in my corner.

For everyone who has ever shared the love of my books… THANK YOU. It truly does mean the world to me.

Melissa Crump- there is a reason you are in this section on every book. I literally couldn't do what I do without your help. You keep me on track, you keep me accountable, and you help me to remember what's important. You are my whip cracker, my shoulder to lean on, and more importantly… my friend. So thank you from the bottom of my butt (it's bigger than my heart) for being the most amazing PA a girl could ask for.

A. Zavarelli's Femme Fatales- thank you for making me smile every day. I love our little Facebook haven.

And to all my readers-

Thank you for taking this journey with me.

xoxo

Ashleigh

Made in the USA
Columbia, SC
22 July 2018